The Quilting Cruise Gambit

The Winslow Quilting Mysteries

Book Five

Jan Cerney

Chapter One

A chilly wind blew across the yellow poppies fluttering on the thawing tundra. Summer had transformed a dark world of ice and snow into a landscape of daylight, bursting forth in purple, pink, and blue blooming wildflowers. Distant snow capped peaks stood as stark sentinels, reminders of a soon to be short-lived summer.

Joe shivered, ignoring the scene in front of him. Not one to appreciate natural beauty, he threw down his pick, snarling at his companion who was mercilessly hacking the ground with the force of a jackhammer. "This is crazy, I wish I'd never let you talk me in to this stupid scheme of yours."

His companion stopped in motion and growled impatiently. "When have I ever led you astray?"

Lots of times, Joe thought to himself but didn't say anything audible.

"You'll change your tune when we start raking in the dough. Besides, I didn't talk you into anything. You came looking for me."

"Yeah," Joe admitted. "This constant daylight doesn't provide any cover. We're like sitting ducks. Not even a tree to hide behind."

Joe had known Otto since high school. Several times he had gotten in trouble by associating with him and helping him in some of his schemes. After he married, his wife put a kibosh on their partnerships. He only agreed to assist him this time because he needed the money. Lately, the bills were piling up. His wife had been sick and wasn't able to work. Otto knew how to make a fast buck if one wasn't worried about bending the law. Joe didn't bother to tell his wife that it was Otto who he was working with this time.

Otto returned to his hacking, yelling over his shoulder. "Who's going to be coming out here in this desolate country anyway?"

"A ranger, that's who."

"So far we haven't seen anyone." Otto waved his arm. "Quit your yammering and get to work."

Joe jerked the black hood from his head, pushed his black hair to the side, so he could see the ground clearly. He was about to heft the pick once again when he noticed his companion had stopped his pursuit and was moving more carefully as he pried something out of the ground. He dropped the pick and rushed over to his blonde, grizzled partner.

"Take a gander at this. It's got to be worth at least several thousand dollars."

"Looks like something only a scientist would be interested in," Joe commented dryly.

"Luckily, a lot of people want one of these."

"Wouldn't it be easier to use hydraulics," Joe, the grumbler complained. 'This pick and shovel work is back-breaking."

"You got the money? Besides, we're not exactly legal here. Can't attract too much attention."

"All we need are high pressure hoses and a generator."

"Too risky."

"It was just a thought." Joe's voice faded off as he tugged at the relic from the past. He didn't like to be reminded that they were on federal land. Somehow Otto was tipped off that this was the best place to find what they were looking for.

After an hour of careful excavation, they pried the object from its ancient grave. "It's a beauty," Otto exclaimed as he tugged with all his strength. "More effort, Joe. I'm not leaving it here for someone else to find."

Joe growled under his breath and used every ounce of muscle he had before they unearthed the treasure that hadn't seen daylight for thousands of years. "It smells rotten."

"Like money you mean. Now to get it on the sled."

"How we going to lift it?"

"Man, you're the most complaining guy I ever met," Otto spewed the words from his mouth. "If I'd known you'd be such a pain, I'd found someone else to come along. Now, get that winch over here."

Joe shrunk back in thought. He hadn't wanted to come, but he felt he had no other choice even if it meant doing something illegal. This was a serious matter, not that he hadn't been picked up for poaching and a few other lesser crimes in the past.

Once the dubious treasure was loaded with a winch, Joe sighed in relief, but Otto turned back to the ground from which it came.

"You going to look for another?"

"Yeah, where's there's one there's got to be more."

"Let's get out of here while we can," Joe protested. "This plus our other stash ought to pay enough for a while."

"I'm not leaving 'til we're sure there are no more. We're not coming back here again. Our luck's about to run out."

Joe jammed his hands into the sweatshirt's pockets and watched as Otto searched for places to dig like a wild dog digging for bones.

Joe followed Otto's barked orders through gritted teeth as the hours dragged by. It was late in the day when Otto finally decided to quit, although the sun would give light continually. "I suggest we call it a day. Maybe try it again tomorrow."

"Tomorrow?" Joe shouted too loudly. "I thought we'd call it quits for good."

Joe ceased complaining when he saw Otto forming his fists into a hard steel ball. He warned himself not to push this explosive man too far. Otto nearly killed a man once in a bar fight when they were young men, and he knew not to push Otto into something he didn't want to do. He held his arms up in compliance. "Okay, sorry, guess I'm just hungry and tired."

Otto slapped him on the back in camaraderie. "Okay old friend, didn't mean to drive you too hard. After a stiff drink and something to fill our belly the day will look better."

For the last several weeks they had set up a camp outside of the federal land about two miles near a river to appear that they were fishing. The dogs pulled the sled easily on the half frozen ground. Joe felt better knowing that Otto had forgiven him for his outbursts. Otto was right, something to drink and food for Joe's growling stomach would make things right again. Surely, Otto would be satisfied with today's find. Added to their other cache, it would appear to be a lucrative haul.

———

The sun still shone brightly as the scrape of the sled approached the camp. An attractive woman peered through the window and saw only one man holding the sled's ropes and guiding the dogs as he hot-footed it across country. She withdrew from the window of the weather-beaten, abandoned shack that looked like oversized packing crates jammed together. She turned her attention to the wood-stove and the ham and bean soup bubbling in a large pot, detesting the job of cooking, but if it meant keeping the peace with Otto she'd do it. Pouring two cans of soup into a pot was worth the inconvenience. Her nose curled at the primitive living conditions she endured for the last several days. After stoking the fire in the cook-stove, she sat down at the table and watched the door. The fragrance of food stirred up hunger pangs. The sound of the sled runners crunching the frozen ground grew louder and then ceased as Otto pulled up near the door. The dogs barked happy yelps when he unhooked them and led them toward their kennels and food.

In fifteen minutes he pushed in the dilapidated door and grinned.

She remained at the table while studying his face. "Did you get it?"

"Yeah, it's on the sled. Want to see it?"

"Not right now."

"We'll add it to our other stash, and we'll be ready to go."

She nodded. "Got soup on the stove."

He struggled with his boots. They hit the floor with a thud. "I'm hungry. Haven't eaten all day."

She reluctantly left her chair and took a large bowl out of the cupboard and ladled in the soup. "Didn't figure you would."

After removing his coat and sweat shirt, reducing his size significantly, he sat down to the meal. "Got our tickets?"

"Of course." She picked them up from under a magazine on the table and held them up for him to see. "One for you and one for me."

Otto looked up at her while spooning the soup into his mouth. "Good girl. Knew I could count on you. Just one more stop before we board."

"Ah, yes."

He slurped his soup and then wiped his mouth with his sleeve. "I suggest we board alone. You can come aboard later along the route."

She wrinkled her nose. "You'd better adjust your table manners if you want to play the part."

His eyes narrowed. "I'll do as I please. Remember, the only reason I asked you along is because of your connections to move the goods."

She laughed. "What about the dogs? Will Joe take care of them?"

Otto dropped his gaze to the table. "Joe? No, he decided to explore the other side of the mountain." He turned to her with a sinister smile. "And since when have you worried about dogs?"

———

Joe frantically grabbed at the partially frozen ground as he tumbled down the ravine. Rocks pounded his skull and scraped his face. Dirt and ice filled his mouth between his screams of pain. He attempted to dig his heels into the ground, but the rate of speed descending the abyss prevented success. He thought about the times he lied to his wife but before confessing his sins, he stopped at the bottom of the canyon with a thud.

He laid there a while, orientating himself to what had just happened. "I must have slipped," he said out loud and craned his neck to see the top of the ridge. Disappointed that he didn't see Otto, he yelled for help until he became hoarse. *Didn't Otto hear him? Where was he anyway?*

Since no one was going to help him, he attempted to stand. The pain in his ankle surged through his body. Dizzy and sick to his stomach, Joe fell to the ground, striking his head. How long he lay there unconscious he didn't know. He felt the lump on his head and groaned with pain.

Still confused as to Otto's disappearance, he willed himself to stand and placed one foot in front of the other. Somehow he must get to the base camp. Otto was probably wondering what happened to him.

His head throbbed, and then he remembered after a streak of pain. Something or was it someone had pushed him from the back. Who could it have been? Otto? No, it couldn't have been. They were partners, but his wife had told him once not to trust Otto.

The fury of the revelation pushed him onward in spite of the injured ankle. Finding an easier way up the ravine propelled him forward. He had to reach base camp or he wouldn't survive. The searing pain in his foot was more than he could bear. His scream of pain came from deep in his soul, and all went black.

Chapter Two

Dora couldn't help but smile to herself as she tidied the kitchen after breakfasting with Milton in their Hedge City home. Like Pandora's Box, a whole new life had opened for her, and she was no longer a spinster as the town's people had labeled her. She noticed the Hedge City populace looked upon her in a different light now that she was married. Gone were the 'I feel sorry for you' glances. She could tell by their whispering smiles, she and Milton were now the topic of conversation. Marrying at the age of sixty plus! She couldn't imagine what they were snickering about. But she didn't care. Life was good.

Milton had errands to run and left her to the task of doing the breakfast dishes. Ordinarily, he helped with the clean-up. Dora had been going out of her way to make something special for their morning meals. She had been trying to impress Milton with her new gourmet recipes. Before they had married, she knew he ate out while on assignments. Never claiming to be a great cook, she wondered if she could measure up to his expectations.

Besides, cooking for an appreciative husband was so different from putting a meal on for a sister. She laughed when she thought of the mornings Josie and she had argued over who was going to cook. Usually, they couldn't agree and settled for a bowl of cereal or a piece of toast. She could even smell the burned toast now. Besides, they both were working women and had to keep to a schedule. Both she and Josie worked outside the home almost their entire lives. She had been a high school English teacher, and Josie had run a public library. Coming home to cooking a meal didn't appeal to either one of them. Therefore, they made do with whatever was the simplest to prepare. She had to admit that they were in a rut when it came to variety. Online recipes were now a boon to her imagination, and

Milton seemed pleased with whatever she conjured up for his discriminating taste.

In fact, everything was so different. She had dreaded changing her life for a male companion, but she had to admit that it wasn't nearly as inconvenient as she thought it would be.

Dora glanced at the clock on the fireplace mantle. It was ten o'clock, a time reserved on Saturday morning to call Josie. Very rarely did they miss calling one another at the designated hour. After opening a window to let in fresh air to remove the bacon aroma, she used the house phone and punched in Josie's number and waited for her to answer.

"Dora, it's so good to hear your voice. I don't know about you, but I miss our daily visits."

"I do, too. Life is different but for the good. Don't you think?"

"I do," Josie gushed. "No regrets here, but I'm excited about the trip our husbands surprised us with. Seeing you again will be a bonus. It's been a long time since Christmas. Are you packed yet?"

"I'm working at it. I don't know what to take for the Alaska weather."

"Me neither. I'd leave your short shorts and halter tops at home," Josie said.

"Oh, be serious. You never change, do you?"

"No, guess that's what Anthony loves about me." Josie giggled. "According to the website, a layered look is advised. That way you can add or subtract the clothing the weather demands."

"Makes sense. I must buy a few more sweaters."

"I've added a few things to my wardrobe, too. I packed sweaters, jackets, slacks, and capris. I believe we need to dress up several times while we are on the cruise."

"So does that mean an evening dress?" Dora asked.

"It does. Too bad we can't go shopping together."

"I know. I've always valued your opinion." Dora sat down at the kitchen table and picked at the edge of her place mat. "Are you used to Iowa by now?"

"Sure, it's not that much different from Nebraska, still got the cornfields and humid weather. How does Milton like our house? I mean your house?"

"He hasn't complained. I don't believe where he lives makes that much difference to him."

"Anthony's letting me redecorate the house. Believe me, it needs it. But don't tell him I said so."

"Adding feminine touches?"

"For sure. It looked like the proverbial bachelor pad. Actually, still does."

Dora laughed. "Milton didn't appreciate my floral bedspread. I had to replace it."

"Have you done any subbing at the school?"

"No, Milton wants me home although I still help Alexia at the daycare from time to time."

"Interesting."

"I've come to know the little tykes. They're not so bad." Dora hesitated. "I would have been a good mother."

"Really? Guess we'll never know."

"It's hard to settle into a mundane routine when we have been on the go for the past couple of years."

"I've been thinking of volunteering somewhere, too, but just think in a week we'll be in Washington State where we'll board our cruise ship. Now that's a trip to look forward to."

"I just hope I don't become seasick." Dora wrinkled her nose.

"I know what you mean. Neither of us has had experience on water."

"Are you forgetting our float trip in Colorado on our first trip?" Dora reminded her.

"As I recall, we didn't get sick, but I bet you had sore knuckles?" Josie laughed. "You held on for dear life."

"Very funny." Dora frowned. "Since it's a quilting cruise, we might be able to keep our mind off the water and on creating a quilt."

"Wasn't that nice of our men to think of a quilting cruise for our first anniversary?"

"It was, especially since our guys aren't on assignment. We'll have them all to ourselves," Dora thought out loud.

"Wow, Dora. You have transformed. I figured you would always be a loner."

"People change," Dora flung the words abruptly.

"From what I've been reading, there are lots of activities aboard ship. I believe we'll be occupied with quilting more than we want. I wonder if the guys knew that when they booked the cruise."

"Probably not, but we have the ports to visit and the evenings, too." Dora ran her fingers through her hair. "We'll be together then. I hope."

"This time we'll be able to spend more time in Seattle since we hurriedly by-passed it on our first trip. I think the Space Needle will be fun," Josie paused. "Have you gotten over your fear of heights?"

"No."

Josie laughed. "Maybe it'll be just Anthony and me visiting the space needle."

"Fine, but I doubt Milton will let me back out."

Chapter Three

Both couples flew separately into Seattle where they met each other with open arms. It had been a while since Christmas. Before that, they had toured the southern states together where both sisters were married in an historic plantation home. It had been an interesting trip discovering the origin of Milton's Civil War Quilt along with two romances that had blossomed into marriage.

Dora and Josie were in tears at the sight of each other. They held each other at arm's length, assessing one another. After all, they had spent the greater portion of their life together and had memorized every line and wrinkle. Dora felt that Josie had gained weight since Christmas as she hugged her, but she looked so radiant with happiness. Dora didn't hold it against her. She, on the other hand, was obsessive about her weight, walking every day to maintain her trim size. Josie still dyed her hair the golden blonde color. Dora's hair was even grayer than a year ago.

"Oh, Dora, you look so wonderful," Josie complimented in her normal gushing manner.

"You're too kind. I know I have more wrinkles and gray hair."

"Oh, that doesn't matter. Milton does wonders for you. I'm so glad you realized he was the one."

True, she had about lost Milton to her own insecurities and fear of a new and different life. Josie was right; Milton was good to and for her. She had been discovering daily how truly wonderful he was.

Milton and Anthony weren't nearly as emotional as their wives. They had just spent several weeks together on assignment, but they shook hands as old friends would. Milton looked the same with his cropped red hair. Anthony, like Josie, had put on weight and his hair appeared to be thinning even more. But as usual Milton was smartly dressed and Anthony, with Josie's guidance, looked schooled in the art of traveling.

Earlier, Josie had made reservations for a two night's stay at a lavish Seattle hotel before they boarded the cruise ship to Alaska. Since both sisters were eager to get home after their first tour that took them to the western states, they had opted not to tour Seattle even though Anthony had encouraged them. Now with husbands as escorts, they were most willing to see what Seattle had to offer.

Since they arrived in Seattle as the day was waning, they took the shuttle to their hotel near the waterfront where they opted to dine in the hotel's restaurant and begin touring the next morning. Settling into a sumptuous meal of seafood, Dora and Josie ignored their husbands and rattled on about their lives apart. Both owed all the changes for simply taking the risk to leave Hedge City, Nebraska, and explore the country.

"It could have ended so differently," Dora remarked.

"But it didn't," Josie reminded her. "We managed to overcome all the obstacles."

The two couples visited for a while longer and then went to their separate rooms, agreeing to meet early the next morning.

While enjoying a light breakfast of fruit and oatmeal, they agreed the Space Needle should be first on their list. Rather than renting a car, Anthony suggested they take a tour on the Hop-on tour trolley to see the sights in down-town Seattle. All agreed, as they were familiar with this type of touring, where they could pick and choose what they wanted to see.

Dora still hadn't gotten over her fear of heights, but she agreed due to being outvoted. However, she tried to change her mind when she learned that the observation deck was 520 feet above ground and the dizzying elevator ride only took 41 seconds to reach the top. Milton was persistent in urging her to confront the challenge. She frowned at his hold on her but willed herself to show him she could do this.

Once they reached the observation deck, they were met by a grandiose view of Puget Sound, the Olympic and Cascade Mountains, and the high peaks of Mt. Baker and Mt. Rainier.

"Now wasn't it worth it?" Milton teased his wife who had latched on his arm and had never let go.

"Yes, it was. I should know by now, one has to take risks or miss out on the nectar of life."

Milton patted her arm. "Now you're talking."

"Shall we find an art gallery to tour?" Anthony asked innocently.

"I should say not." Dora was quick with the negative response.

Everyone laughed except Dora and Josie. The sisters still harbored fear of art museums. On their first trip to Chicago and then west to the coast they had discovered art had been stolen from the art galleries that they had just visited. And furthermore, both ladies were accompanied by the art thieves on Amtrak. They even traveled with them in rental cars without suspicion.

Instead of art museums, Josie suggested Pike Place Market near the waterfront. "We can browse the seafood market, sample Seattle cuisine all in a two-hour walking tour."

Anthony winked at Josie. "Sounds like fun to me."

Once they arrived at the market, Dora commented that Pike Place reminded her of San Francisco's wharf.

"It sure does," Josie agreed. "It has the same fishy smell. I believe we were hoping not to meet up with you Anthony when we visited the wharf in the Golden Gate city?" She laughed.

"I can't believe you ladies thought we were the bad guys. And now look at us. We're married."

As they watched the fish purveyors tossing fish back and forth to each other, Anthony answered a call on his phone. He spoke for a while before he ended the conversation. Dora noticed he appeared troubled.

"What is it?" Milton asked. "Something wrong?"

Anthony frowned. "Something to upset our plans."

"How?" Josie paled.

"It's about our last assignment. It seems we are being called back to testify."

"Can't it wait?" Milton challenged. "Or change the date?"

"We can't get our cruise money back at this late date! Can we?" Josie sputtered in disbelief.

Milton ran his fingers through his cropped, red hair in thought. "How long must we be gone?"

"Just for a couple of days. We must leave today," Anthony answered.

Milton took command of the situation. "Okay then. I suggest you gals board the cruise ship as planned, and we'll make arrangements to join you in a few days."

Dora scowled. "Are you serious?"

"I am. Cruise ships are safer than staying here in a city. And like you said, we'd be out all our money."

"Oh, this is terrible," Josie wailed. "I don't want to leave without you."

"It will be fine," Anthony consoled. "Now, to make arrangements. First, getting you to back to the hotel. Next making plane reservations."

Milton gently pulled Dora to him. "Don't worry. The two days will go by in a hurry. And besides, what could happen on a cruise ship?"

Chapter Four

Otto had taken time to clean up before he arrived in Seattle. He shaved, got a haircut, and donned new clothes before he drove his rented truck straight to a warehouse on the wharf where sea birds squawked and dipped around the dock workers. A man in a blue sweatshirt met him and guided him to an unloading dock. Several others dressed in work clothes bustled about to help remove the cargo packed in crates from the truck.

The man in blue admonished the help to work quickly and gestured to Otto with thumbs up. "Nice haul."

Otto smiled. "Now to get orders and move this stuff pronto."

"I've a special delivery for you." The man in blue handed him a black suitcase with an envelope.

Otto opened the case and sorted through the contents. "And how am I supposed to get this on board?"

"Just flash the envelope I gave you. We have someone stationed at the check in. There will be no problem."

Otto closed the suitcase and put the envelope in his pocket.

"Read the letter before you get on the ship."

Otto nodded and picked up the suitcase and left the truck at the dock. He walked several blocks before he called a taxi to take him to the pier where the cruise ship to Alaska was waiting. He then unloaded one beige bag and the black suitcase, and wheeled them to the boarding area. While waiting in line, Otto scrutinized the two women who were in queue ahead of him. He heard them lamenting about having to board the ship without their husbands and laughed at their predicament to himself, thinking this must be their first cruise.

As he neared the check in, he removed the envelope from his pocket and held it, so it would be seen. Before he had time to worry, a young man, who appeared to be no stranger to a gym, swiped the suitcase from his hand. He briefly examined it and then placed it with the others bags that would be delivered to the assigned rooms. Otto protested that he wanted to keep the black suitcase, but the man who checked him in assured him all would be well. Otto placed the envelope back in his pocket, remembering he hadn't taken the time to read the note. The ladies were still in line ahead of him, and he heard them again, babbling about their predicament.

———

"I'm so bummed that we must board a cruise ship all by ourselves," Josie complained. "Just when we thought everything was going our way, Anthony and Milton are called away on assignment."

"But they said they would join us in a couple of days," Dora reminded her as she rammed into the man ahead of her. "Oh, my excuse me," she apologized.

"The cruise only lasts seven days," Josie told her curtly. "And when did they ever solve a case in a couple of days?"

"They're testifying, not solving anything."

"I know," Josie groaned. "We must make the best of it. We have no choice. Let's find our rooms and take the luggage inside. The bags should be waiting by the doors in awhile."

"We'd better take our time. The bags can't be delivered that fast."

After the line of passengers checked in, they fanned out at the grand Atrium, the focal point of the ship's opulence and promise of grand entertainment.

"Wow isn't this beautiful," Josie exclaimed, titling her head upwards to see the multiple tiers of the cruise ship overlooking the atrium. "First class I'd say." She steadied herself by grabbing on to Dora's arm.

Chandeliers, a glass elevator, polished chrome and soft lighting made Dora's eyes pop. "Almost sinful. Isn't it?"

Dora and Josie read the map guides by the elevators, confident about their traveling expertise. But before they were able to decipher the location of their rooms, they both were feuding over what direction they were supposed to go. "Why is this so confusing," Josie fumed.

"Something to do with the forward and aft of the ship."

After several attempts at the correct direction, they finally found their ocean view window rooms. As instructed earlier, they saw their delivered luggage by the doors of the cabins. "At least we are next door to one another," Dora pointed out as she unlocked the door and picked up one of her suitcases and carried it into the cabin. She surveyed their cozy room and walked around the bed to peek out the window and then returned for the rest of the luggage. Seeing Josie outside her door, Dora suggested that they find their way to the deck to experience the bon voyage party as they left the harbor.

"We'll unpack later," Dora told her sister as she attempted to haul in the black nondescript bag. "I don't remember this bag being so heavy," Dora groaned under the weight. "Did you put something else in here?"

"No, I never touched it. Here let me help you," Josie offered, pushing the black inert object as Dora pulled.

"I should check and see what's in here," Dora said all out of breath. "Maybe Milton added something at the last minute without telling me."

"Later. Let's hurry to the deck before we miss our bon voyage party."

Josie barged out of the room to tour the ship with Dora close behind. "But which way do we go?" Dora asked winded with the effort.

"Gosh I don't know."

"We should have left a trail of bread crumbs," Dora suggested in jest.

"Let's simply go back the way we came and look for directions to the deck. After several turns and backtracks, the sisters walked out on the deck to join the myriad of passengers just as the ship was edging away from the dock. Most of the passengers were sipping pink drinks with umbrellas perched on the rims of their souvenir glasses. Others waved farewell to anyone who was watching the departure.

"Isn't this grand?" Josie said, giddy with excitement. "I only wish Anthony was here with me."

"I know how you're feeling. A romantic cruise without our husbands. Drat our luck."

"Just like *The Love Boat*," Josie said. "Only no love for us."

"The receding Seattle skyline is beautiful. I suppose we should take pictures of each other to show the fellows."

"Sure why not."

Josie pointed to a waiter balancing a tray. "Oh, Dora, look at those appetizing pink beverages they're selling in souvenir glasses. Ooh, I want one."

"I'm certain they have alcohol in them."

"Ah, just one won't hurt." Josie waved to the waiter who immediately added the charge to her card. She sipped the cool, citrus concoction through a straw and smacked her lips in delight while twirling the small decorative yellow umbrella in her hand. "Listen to the music coming from the lido deck. Let's party." Josie led her sister to the action.

Dora sighed, wishing the men were here, so Anthony could take control of his wife.

"I'm going to enjoy this floating palace," Josie said with a smile.

"I'm thinking we should have selected a cruise ship more apropos to our age," Dora said wryly.

"I don't think there is such a ship, besides, not all ships have quilting cruises."

After Josie had enough of the bon voyage celebration, the sisters took another tour of the deck. They breathed in the salty sea air and watched the ocean as it rippled past the stern. "This is one big boat. A floating city," Josie commented. "Let's see what else we have to enjoy for a week."

"And get lost in the process," Dora warned.

"As long as we don't fall overboard we will be alright." Josie's eyes dropped to the ocean below them and shivered.

Dora peered at the ocean from a safe distance, thinking it could happen. "So, do you think people fall overboard?"

"I have heard of that happening before."

After the required emergency drill, the sisters toured the inside of the ship, marveling at the exquisite features of elegance highlighted by an array of lights. They revisited the atrium and watched the elevator encased in a glass tube smoothly carrying passengers up and down to the ship's multiple levels.

"Let's give the elevator a try," Josie suggested to Dora. She agreed and they glided effortlessly. They chose to stop at the shops and looked around.

"Let's save our money for the ports-of-call," Dora advised her sister.

"Good idea. But it does attempt one to buy something beforehand."

The sisters searched out the dining areas, restaurants, the lounges, and fitness areas. "Everything you'd want," Josie commented. "We can even exercise if we want."

Dora groaned. "Don't remind me. After we eat all the wonderful food available, we'll have to or the guys won't recognize us."

"Look on the bright side. We don't have to cook for a week."

"Good point."

"Oh and there's even dancing," Josie said, noticing couples out on the dance floor. Her exuberance diminished. "But no one to dance with."

Dora sniffed. "I don't really want to dance, anyway."

"What a ship," Josie said as they approached their cabins. "Are you up to formal dining this evening or do you want to pick and choose from all the food venues available throughout the ship?"

"We signed up for early seating, didn't we?"

"We did. Let's dress for the formal dinner. I want to wear some of the stylish clothes I bought."

"But we're without escorts, remember?"

"Women don't need escorts now-a-days. If we must, we'll explain our husbands will join us later. Besides, it will give us a chance to meet new people," Josie said.

"You know how I feel about new people. And don't let anyone know our husbands are detectives. If word gets around, the passengers will clam up and distrust us. It's better to be privy to gossip."

"I know you are uncomfortable around strangers, but haven't you learned to climb out of your shell yet? I thought by now Milton would have taught you to be more sociable. And what about the epiphany you experienced over Christmas. You know. Befriending strangers?"

"Overcoming my inhibitions is difficult." Dora glared. "But just to prove I'm willing to be agreeable, I'll consent. We'll see with whom we are assigned for a week of formal dining."

"That a girl." Josie patted her shoulder. "Meet you in an hour. Your door or mine?"

"Mine. We'll unpack in the meantime."

Dora kicked off her shoes as soon as she entered her cabin. She walked around the double bed and peered out the window at the ocean. Never fond of water, she didn't permit herself to dwell on the large expanse of ocean separating her from terra firma. So far, she didn't feel any ill effects from the ocean waves. In fact, the water seemed calm and lulled her into a sense of well-being. A nap appealed to her just then, but unpacking beckoned her. She began with her large suitcase by taking out her wardrobe and hanging up each piece in the closet provided. She marveled how well the space was used in the compact but cozy room.

Her last piece of baggage was on the floor where she and Josie dragged it in. Curious why it felt so heavy, she sat on the floor to unzip the case. It unzipped harder than she remembered but with one extra tug she completed the task. She lifted the lid and shut it before she had a good look. "What!" she shouted to herself. She sat stunned for a moment and then lifted the tag on the handle. Her name was not on the identifying label. In fact, no name was written on it. She gingerly assumed standing position and charged out of the room and knocked on Josie's door.

"Let me in." Dora pounded.

"What's the matter?" Josie answered. "I was just about to get in the shower."

"Come to my room. I got the wrong suitcase."

Josie wrapped her robe tightly around her. "So exchange it for yours."

"You got to see what's in it."

"A dead body?" Josie asked in all seriousness.

"No, yes. I don't know. Something weird."

"Maybe we should call security," Josie suggested, becoming alarmed.

"I'm not sure what to do."

"Call Milton," Josie ordered.

"But it's expensive to call from a ship and besides we can't always get a connection," Dora protested. "And he's probably still in the air."

"You're going to worry about a few dollars at a time like this?" Josie asked incredulously and then calmed. "Let's see what you found first." Josie followed Dora to her cabin. "Then you can call."

Once inside Dora's cabin the sisters bent over the suitcase as Dora slowly lifted the lid. Josie wrinkled her nose at the musty odor. What is this stuff? It's not alive, is it? Poke it and see."

"I'm not going to poke it," Dora insisted in horror. "It looks like a heap of …of I don't know what." Her face contorted into disgust.

Josie bent closer. "I would say it's like something petrified."

"It doesn't appear like anything I have seen before."

"Bones, trees, plants can be petrified," Josie pointed out. "Didn't we have a petrified turtle in our yard once?" Josie walked around the suitcase and viewed the contents from all angles. "Take a picture and send it to Milton and Anthony."

"Humans can be petrified, too?" Dora's hands shook as she fumbled with her phone and took several pictures of the mass of unidentified matter.

"Push send and see what the fellows say."

"I don't want to be alone with this suitcase," Dora stated adamantly. "What if the owner knocks on my door?"

Josie scowled. "Answer the door."

"I'd rather not."

Josie heaved a sigh of disgust. "Bring your clothes and come to my cabin, then. Hopefully the guys will call us back soon."

While Josie showered, Dora kept her eyes on her phone, hoping Milton would respond before they left for dinner. How would she be able to eat, knowing that strange suitcase was in her room? And why wasn't there a name on it. It did appear similar to her luggage, so that explained the mix-up. And where was her suitcase? She must inquire if her suitcase was returned. Perhaps she could find out who returned it and clear up the mistake.

Dora could barely wait until Josie finished her shower, so she could tell her of her plan. "Let the authorities figure this out," Josie advised her. "In fact, let's just report it and not bother to wait for a message. The guys could be too busy to respond."

"I might be overreacting. I could probably straighten this out on my own and not embarrass myself with Milton."

Josie placed her hands on her hips. "Why would you embarrass yourself with Milton?"

"He's strong and brave. I don't want to seem like a ninny, afraid of my own shadow."

"But we were and maybe still are," Josie said.

"Not so much anymore. Don't you think we have become more confident?"

"We have, but that doesn't mean you need to solve a case on your own. We don't have that kind of training," Josie protested as she plugged in her hair dryer.

"I can at least inquire about my suitcase. Then we will see where it leads us."

"Us? Do you want to sleep with that suitcase in your room while you figure out this mystery?"

"Not really, but you offered me a space in your cabin."

Josie plopped down on the bed and vigorously towel dried her hair, releasing a strawberry scent. "So what's your plan?"

"I'm going to ask before dinner and see if my suitcase has been returned."

"Are you going to mention the one in your room?"

Dora narrowed her eyes. "No, I'll keep it a secret for now until Milton returns my message."

Josie's eyes grew wide. "Are you thinking we have stumbled onto something illegal, again?" Josie asked.

"You know our luck," Dora sighed heavily. "It seems we attract thieves as soon as we leave home."

———

Otto wasn't interested in touring the ship only anxious in finding his room and the black bag. He had cruised before and had little difficulty locating his quarters down a long hallway. He noticed a few of the bags had already been delivered at several doors, but before he removed his own bags in front of his cabin, he peered over his shoulder to see if anyone was near. The hall was mostly empty. He unlocked his door before wheeling the beige and black suitcase into his cabin, immediately noticing that the black bag pulled effortlessly. He checked the tag and cursed under his breath. This was the wrong cabin number and realized that his suitcase must have been confused with the one delivered to his room.

He slumped on the edge of the bed, contemplating what he should do. The cabin number wasn't too far from his room. There wasn't much time to waste. If someone opened his suitcase or took it to the main desk, he would have explaining to do. But maybe the occupant of the cabin hadn't even noticed he or she had the wrong suitcase. Without further thought, he left his cabin and dashed down the hall to the other cabin. He knocked on the door several times, finally concluding the cabin was vacant. Rubbing the back of his neck in thought, he toyed with the idea of leaving a note but dismissed it. It was best not to be associated with the black bag.

Once back inside his quarters, he set the black suitcase on his bed and unzipped it. Angry with the mix-up, he quickly sorted through the clothes for a clue but found nothing except that the suitcase belonged to a woman.

———

Anticipating their first formal dining aboard ship, Dora and Josie dressed in formal long dresses. Dora wore a sapphire blue skirt and tunic that she had purchased in Seattle before the cruise. Josie splurged and bought several formal garments of which she asked Dora's opinion.

"Wear the turquoise one," Dora suggested. "Then you can wear the Arizona jewelry you bought on our first trip."

"Good idea. I'll save the sparkly gold one when Anthony joins us."

As soon as the ladies decided they appeared presentable and spritzed on their favorite floral perfume, they locked their cabin doors and ventured out to search for their dining room. On their way, they stopped at the information desk to inquire concerning Dora's suitcase. Apologizing profusely, the staff checked their records and determined her suitcase had not been returned but to come back again the next day. Dora didn't mention the unwanted bag in her possession.

"This is strange," Dora commented. "Surely someone by now has noticed he or she has the wrong bag."

"Not necessarily," Josie consoled. "Who would need the contents of the strange bag in your room for any reason on this cruise?"

"You're right. But what does this person want with petrified stuff on a cruise?"

"Perhaps a conference for paleontologists or something," Josie conjectured.

"Plausible guess. Maybe, I should research a possible conference in Alaska."

"What did you have packed in your suitcase? Not your medications I hope."

"No, my shoes and a few jackets. I do have one coat in my other suitcase until I'm able to buy another if I don't find my luggage."

"Don't you want to get your suitcase back?"

"Well, yes. But I don't want the person that owns the black suitcase to know who I am. Has it crossed your mind we could be dealing with stolen goods?"

Josie eyes widened. "Well if it is, then I don't understand your reasoning. Check tomorrow again and see if someone returned a black suitcase."

"Maybe." Suddenly Dora gestured for Josie to stop talking. "Wait. I have a message on my phone." Dora quickly opened Milton's message. It was short and to the point. She hurriedly read that Milton advised her to report the suitcase to security. To him and Anthony it appeared to be a type of fossils. He would research the contents later. At the moment Milton and Anthony were busy and were trying to speed up testifying in order to join the ladies on the cruise. Dora turned to Josie and frowned.

"What's the matter? I think Milton's advice is right on the mark. Give the suitcase over to someone trained to deal with such matters. Now let's eat. I'm looking forward to something scrumptious. Cruise ships are noted for their food."

The waiter seated the sisters at a large table with three couples. Introductions were made, and the sisters explained that their husbands were detained with business but would join them later. Josie did most of the talking while Dora analyzed their dining companions. The men were dressed in suits and noted Milton would fit in perfectly with this group. The women were attired in long dresses.

Their impeccably dressed waiter appeared to be of oriental descent and introduced himself as Tron.

A middle-aged couple, Janelle and Don, seated to Dora's right, appeared affable and were clearly enjoying their fourth cruise, according to their conversation. Janelle's black dress was a little low-cut for Dora's taste, but she wore it well. Seasoned with traveling, the couple offered advice to Josie and Dora on what to see and how to get the most from the ports-of-call.

Dora thought that the retired couple, Bridgett and Bill, behaved aloof to the fellow diners. She guessed them to be quite affluent from the glittering diamonds Bridgett wore on each hand. Her diamond necklace complemented her shimmering silver dress as well. Flashes of a possible jewelry heist entered Dora's mind, but she shook off the notion. To Dora, the couple seemed to be either bored with cruising or, perhaps like her, they weren't interested in mingling.

The final couple sat to Dora's left. She thought Ted and Alicia were quite interesting. They had traveled extensively and collected regional artworks that they displayed in a museum of which they were the curators. It was with them that Dora exchanged conversation, especially when they discussed Alaskan art. Dora felt comfortable with the couple. Alicia didn't seem pretentious as she wore a simple long skirt and green blouse of a crinkly material. Her jewelry consisted of carved white figures. Dora didn't want to stare or ask of their origin, afraid of revealing her lack of knowledge. She wasn't able to ask many questions before the meal was served and the discussion rotated to different topics, but she made a mental note she would ask them more about Alaska later.

Dora noticed Josie relishing each meal course the reserved waiter served her. She had ordered scampi with garlic butter and had to admit the formal meal was indeed delicious, but she wasn't too thrilled about making small talk with everyone seated at the table. But if she wanted to see Ted and Alicia again she must commit herself to formal dining every evening.

When the meal concluded, Dora and Josie strolled upon the deck before retiring to their cabins. A slight breeze rustled their long skirts. Dora pulled a white lace jacket around her shoulders. Dora had momentarily forgotten about the strange suitcase and concentrated on the stars, thinking that they radiated brighter where nothing obstructed their brilliance.

"Now I have a little understanding how the navigators must have felt," Josie speculated.

"I for one would not have ventured out on high seas with no guarantee of returning to where I started with only the stars to guide me," Dora said flatly.

"Do you still want to bunk with me?" Josie asked.

"If you don't mind, I would," Dora replied. "It's so lonely without Milton."

"What are you going to do about the strange suitcase?"

"I don't know. Guess I'll deal with it in the morning."

"Want to check and see if the strange baggage is still in your room before you retire?"

"Why wouldn't it be?"

Josie shrugged. "Someone might have traced it to you and broke in to retrieve it, especially if it's stolen."

"Never thought of that. Perhaps we should hide it. Bring it to your room."

"But I thought the contents made you uneasy?"

"Like Milton said, it's just fossils. They're dead."

"Alright," Josie agreed. "Let's get the uninvited bag to my room."

Dora unlocked the door of her cabin and entered to a well-lit room.

"Who turned the light on?" Josie blurted in panic.

"Me. I turned the lamp on before I left."

Josie cringed and let out a long sigh. "Oh, I didn't know."

Dora laughed. "Are you spooked?"

Josie ignored her comment. "Let's heft this bag and move it to my room."

Both sisters latched onto the handle and dragged it to Josie's cabin. "This is one bag that should have more wheels," Dora complained, puffing.

"I hope we can get this mystery solved soon. I want to enjoy the cruise rather than speculate why we have this suitcase in our possession."

"I intend to do just that," Dora said with conviction. She changed into her matching cobalt blue nightgown and robe, then sat on the edge of her bed, took out her phone and researched a possible paleontology conference in Alaska.

"Finding anything?" Josie called from the bathroom.

"No conference that I can see."

"Then why is there a suitcase of fossils aboard ship and in our room?"

Chapter Five

The next day, Dora and Josie breakfasted early at one of the convenient breakfast bars in order to arrive at their quilt sign-up at nine o'clock. Sizzling crisp bacon appealed to Dora that morning. She ordered it with scrambled eggs. Josie, on the other hand, settled on a waffle with whipped cream and strawberries.

On this particular cruise the sisters would complete a quilt commemorating their Alaska journey. Since they would be cruising the first day at sea, the quilt classes would begin shortly. They had already selected their design a month earlier.

"I suppose we must split up since we chose a different design," Josie said to her sister who popped bacon into her mouth.

Dora hurriedly chewed and swallowed. "I'm happy we chose to do something different, although we won't be able to spend much time together."

"We'll meet other people that way," Josie reminded her. "Someone aboard owns that suitcase."

"You think that someone is in our quilting class?"

"Could be."

"Now you're thinking like a detective, but I'm not sure who we are looking for." Secretly she hoped she had learned how to be observant from Milton.

Josie hunched her shoulders. "I don't want to think like a detective. I'm just saying it won't hurt to pay attention."

"I suppose you have something there," Dora said unsure of her abilities.

Josie grimaced. "We need Anthony and Milton. I'd rather just have a good time."

After navigating haphazardly through the ship, Dora and Josie entered a large room with sewing tables and machines. Various wall hangings adorned the walls displaying the myriad

Alaskan themed possibilities. The quilting staff cordially welcomed all the prospective quilters and introduced them to the options available. "The instructors have impeccable credentials," Josie whispered to Dora after she perused the brochure.

"They certainly have. I'm impressed," Dora said while glancing around at the quilt designs displayed. "I do like the one called Northern Lights."

Josie nodded. "I adore the one called Glacier Bay. Both of them say Alaska to me."

The instructors separated the group into different classes. Dora felt confident she could handle any pattern that she selected. She sighed in relief when she was handed a kit with pre-cut pieces. In addition, the sewing machines they were to use were new, and luckily she was familiar with the brand. This will be a snap, she said to herself. She hoped Josie felt as confident as she was.

The kit contained an array of colorful squares to mimic the northern lights and several appliqué pieces of Alaska scenes. Her days with Sophie Wainwright in Cooperstown, constructing the author quilt, had prepared her for any appliqué challenges. She briefly recalled the hours spent cutting the shapes resembling houses and appliquéing them to a background. It was a huge commitment to fulfill practically a stranger's wish.

The machines hummed in unison as the participants joined the pieces together after instruction from their sewing leader. Dora barely had any time to notice the women around her. All were intent on accomplishing as much as they could in the time allotted. Keeping on schedule deterred an overabundance of chatter.

During the mid-morning break, Dora introduced herself to the women who were seated next to her. Each took her turn in giving her name and where she was from. None were from Nebraska. To Dora, they seemed like typical women interested in quilting and traveling, except for a willowy woman from New

York who wanted to know every detail of Dora's life. She didn't seem like a quilter type but overall Dora thought nothing suspicious about the participants, but then she remembered when she traveled with art thieves on their first trip, thinking they were ordinary people. I should have learned my lesson, she thought to herself. Some people are very good at masking who they really are.

At lunch break, Dora rejoined Josie at the sumptuous buffet. "How does one choose from all this beautiful food," Josie asked without expecting an answer.

"We have six days to sample everything," Dora reminded her in her big sister tone. "Don't over stuff yourself."

After have selecting a sampling of several items, the sisters choose a table by the window overlooking the ocean, undulating in gentle waves. A few sea birds hopped on the crests of water for a ride. "I haven't been the least bit seasick, have you?" Josie asked while beginning with her salad.

"I haven't, either, but my bed seemed to rock me to sleep last night. I wonder what would happen if we experience rough water?"

"Ooh, let's not think of that possibility. I fear I wouldn't do too well."

"How's your quilt coming?" Dora asked after pouring on more salad dressing.

"Great. No problem at all. I love the blues we are using. Of course, blue is considered a cool color and when put the design is put together I imagine it will appear like snow and ice, hence glaciers."

"Tomorrow is a stop in Juneau. No sewing that day."

"A break will be nice, though," Josie mused. "I look forward to taking in the history." She laughed. "Anthony would have made sure of that."

"What tour did we sign up for?"

"It was the one with a tour of Juneau as well as the glacier. I'm anxious to see glaciers especially when I'm trying to reproduce one on cloth."

"So far everything we've seen is beautiful."

"I agree. Wish the fellows were with us to share it."

"Shall we dine formal tonight?"

"I don't see why not." Josie faced Dora. "Do you have objections?"

"No, I don't. I'd like to visit with Ted and Alicia again. They seem to know quite a bit about Alaskan culture, artifacts, and such."

"I overheard that they operate a museum."

"They do. I'd like to find out more. What do you think about the other couples?"

"I'd rather not make snap judgments. So far they seem okay to me."

"Have you noticed anyone unusual in your class?" Dora asked.

"I haven't met many ladies yet, but I did see Alicia and Janelle. Didn't talk to them, though. And you?'

"No, too early to tell, I suppose. Besides, I think fossils are a man's occupation, don't you?"

Josie squared her shoulders. "Not necessarily. Women can be scientists, too."

"Perhaps, but what if that suitcase belongs to a man?"

Josie peered at her quizzically. "Would it be a problem?"

"Yes. How are we supposed to meet men? We're married."

"Oh, I see what you mean. Another reason to turn the suitcase over to the authorities."

Dora ignored her advice and glanced at her watch. "Lunch break is nearly over."

"But I haven't had dessert yet," Josie protested.

"Have a treat tonight."

"But did you see all the choices on the buffet? I saw chocolate pudding, a triple layer chocolate cake."

Dora shrugged. "Anthony will thank you for skipping dessert. Meet you in the lobby after class." Secretly, Dora regretted missing dessert, too. The cheese cake looked divine, but more importantly, Josie's comment about turning the suitcase over to the ship's personnel made sense.

After sewing class dismissed, the sisters chatted about what they would wear for evening dining while on their way to their cabins. Josie had brought along several formal outfits, but Dora had limited herself to one. Josie decided on her turquoise gown, and Dora settled on black slacks and her silver sequined blouse which complemented her graying hair beautifully.

Dora opened the door to her cabin first and let out a scream before Josie reached her own. Josie turned abruptly and froze when she saw her sister's face as she retreated from her cabin. "Dora what is it," she asked feebly without taking a step toward her.

"Somebody has been in my room. They literally tore it apart."

Josie inched forward and peered inside to see the bureau drawers opened, the sheets stripped from the beds, and clothes strewn from the closet. "Why would someone do such a thing?"

Dora trembled. "I don't know, unless…unless they were looking for something? Like…like the suitcase or the contents."

"We need to report this right away."

Dora pulled her into the room and closed the door. "Not so fast. Let's think a minute."

Josie's face turned pale. "What's there to think about? Someone broke into your room."

"But they didn't take anything?" Dora protested.

"Are you sure?"

"What do I have they would want? My few pieces of costume jewelry?"

"How about money?"

"I took it to your cabin last night."

Josie's face crinkled into panic. "My cabin may not be safe anymore. We've got to get rid of that suitcase. Maybe they broke into my room, too."

"Let's check." Dora pulled her along and unlocked Josie's door. Dora cracked the door and peeked inside. Finding nothing disturbed, she motioned for Josie it was okay to enter. She closed the door and went immediately to the hidden suitcase. It was still where she had left it. "Open it," Josie demanded. Dora lifted the lid and the contents were as they had left them as well as the same musty smell.

"Dora, please give up this insane idea of solving the case on your own," Josie pleaded. "Whoever owns the suitcase is desperate to find it. It must be valuable, and furthermore they don't want anyone to know they are the owners."

"You're right. Otherwise, they would have reported it as missing. But on the bright side, they might not have connected us as together."

"You're mad," Josie blared. "Give up this silly notion. And have you considered that our lives might be in danger?"

Dora paced the small space. "We must get rid of the suitcase, but where?"

"Give it to the authorities," Josie shouted.

"Have you considered they might not believe us? Perhaps, we have waited too long. For sure, they will want to know why we waited until now to tell them."

"Right, I never thought of that." Josie frowned. "Message the guys. Ask them when they can join us. I fear we are over our heads at this moment."

"I will, but until they come, we must hide the bizarre contents."

"We can't hide anything in our cabins."

Dora grinned. "Maybe not, but I have an idea where."

Josie rolled her eyes. "I shouldn't ask. Where?"

"Have you forgotten our storage compartments in the sewing room? We are able to lock them."

Josie glanced at Dora in horror. "You got to be kidding. You want to hide fossils in our sewing lockers?"

"It's the ideal place until Milton and Anthony join us."

"Have you considered the guys will be furious with us for not turning in the suitcase when we found it?"

"It's crossed my mind, but it's too late to turn back now." Dora shrugged. "Let's dress for dinner and then take the contents out of the suitcase, place them in two bags and lock them up for the night."

"Someone could be watching us."

"We'll put the fossils in our handbags and dine first. By then we may not seem suspicious to whomever maybe watching us."

"What about the suitcase?"

Dora squinted in thought. "I'm not sure. How about the laundry room? I'll wrap it up in laundry and leave it there."

"Oh, this plan of yours is insane. Usually, I'm the gutsy one, but this time you've topped the cake."

"Quickly, get ready, so we can leave as soon as possible. I have a feeling someone could pay your cabin a visit, too. I suggest you spend the night with me."

"You mean they're going to dismantle my room, too?"

"Quite possibly."

Josie moaned.

Both Dora and Josie dressed in record time and then sorted through the suitcase. "I think we should have done this first before we dressed," Josie complained, wrinkling her nose.

Dora muttered sisterly advice. "Just be careful. We can always wash our hands."

Dora assumed the lead in investigating the contents. Using her comb, she careful poked around to ascertain the safety of the venture. When nothing snapped at her finger or issued a warning ticking, she became more aggressive in removing the unwanted substance. The first layer contained the odd looking fossil appearing matter. Dora scrunched her face as she lifted the pieces out of the case. She divided the first level between two plastic bags. But as she dug down deeper she let out a sound of surprise and held up a hard white material seemingly cut in different shapes. "What's this?" Dora handed it to Josie who hadn't even touched anything yet. "Go on, it's not going to hurt you."

Josie held it in her hand and using her thumb, she rubbed the smoothness of the object. "I'm not sure, but isn't this ivory. The kind they use for scrimshaw?"

Dora lifted more out of the case and examined the differing shapes. "I believe you're right. But what is this doing with the odd looking stuff?"

"Elephant ivory is illegal? Isn't it?" Josie said unsure of what she said.

"If what we're holding is illegal, somebody is in big trouble."

"I hope it's not us."

Using their largest handbags, the women stuffed in the contents and did their best to balance the heavy load without looking suspicious. Josie grumbled the entire time, berating her sister's poor judgment. For the time being, they left the empty suitcase in Josie's room.

No one was in the hallway when they exited their cabins. Walking as straight and tall as the weighty packs allowed, the sisters hurried to their dining room. Dora felt flush when they arrived, and Josie's cheeks looked feverishly hot. Dora breathed in deeply in an attempt to calm herself. She slipped into the chair next to Alicia whom she noticed was wearing matching earrings and necklace of what she thought to be scrimshaw etched into the same blank pieces of ivory that they had just discovered. Her heart beat wildly as she looked over to Josie who didn't seem to notice. Instead, Josie seemed to be discussing quilt patterns with both Janelle and Alicia.

After the group ordered and perfunctorily chatted about the day, Dora waited for just the right moment to compliment Alicia on her jewelry. "Is that scrimshaw you are wearing," Dora said before Josie could ask her another question about quilting. "I don't' know much about that type of art, but it's very pretty." She hoped Alicia would elaborate on the art form.

"Thank you, I had someone make it for me. I chose the design."

Dora waited for more, but Alicia turned her attention to another question from the senior couple. Bridgett wanted to know where she could buy ivory jewelry. "I like to purchase regional trinkets whenever I can," she said. Alicia told her scrimshaw jewelry was widely available in Alaska.

Dora chided herself on being ignorant about the scrimshaw. She hadn't once even given a thought on purchasing any. It was unique but something that hadn't appealed to her.

Their conversation became most interesting, especially when they discussed the legality of using ivory. Dora leaned into the group even though she hadn't asked the questions. Alicia said that elephant ivory was illegal to use but that Alaska and Siberia had large reserves of ancient woolly mammoth ivory tusks buried under the tundra that was being used for commercial purposes. She told them that the laws were complicated. "People dig for it where it's legal. The Native peoples find the reserves when on their hunting trips. Interested parties can buy the ivory from them."

Josie was drawn into the conversation and propped her elbows on the table. "Fascinating. Are the tusks in fragments?"

Finally, Dora thought in impatience, Josie was catching on.

Alicia continued. "The entire tusk can often be found in the tundra regions of Alaska and Siberia where the permafrost preserves them quite well. Fragments are more common."

"The permafrost melts?" Josie inquired.

"The top layer does in the summer, and that's when the digging takes place."

"Do the mammoth tusks look like elephant tusks?" Josie asked innocently.

"The shape is the same. But since they are so old, mammoth ivory appears like driftwood," Alicia explained. "But they are turned into beautiful ivory with the proper attention."

Dora and Josie exchanged glances. Alicia's description fit the contents in their handbags exactly. Dora couldn't wait to talk to Josie.

———

As soon as the meal concluded, the group split company. Dora had wanted to visit with Alicia further, but she disappeared with her husband. Dora winced at their abrupt departure. She wanted to know more about ivory. Without saying anything to her sister, Dora took a hold of Josie's hand and left for the sewing room.

"Now we know what we have," Josie whispered. "I see why the owners are so intent on getting it back without telling us who they are, especially if we have elephant ivory."

"We're dealing with someone breaking the law."

Josie cringed. "And we have the goods in our possession."

Dora turned the door knob to the sewing room and sighed in relief when she was able to enter. Taking out her key, she opened her sewing cubicle, took out the bag, and stuffed it in with her sewing project and relocked the door. After Josie did the same, the sisters peeked out before they closed the door.

"Now what shall we do?" Josie asked as soon as they were far from the sewing room.

"We need to research mammoth ivory."

"Doing an online search might be too expensive, and it could be traced back to us." Josie noted.

"Remember, we're innocent," Dora reminded her. "There is a library here on ship."

"Will someone be watching us?"

"We must take the chance. Maybe they'll approach us and ask where the ivory is."

"I wish they would, so we could enjoy our cruise. I don't like sneaking around like criminals."

"I'm with you there. Let's check the directory and find the library."

"Should we change first?"

"No, not now. I want to find out more about the ivory."

As expected, the library catered to books on Alaska. Without too much searching, Dora found an article on woolly mammoth ivory. "I never knew this source of ivory existed," Dora told Josie in awe. "Did you?"

"Me neither. What does it say?" She scooted closer to Dora in order to read along with her.

"It says much of what Alicia told us, except she didn't mention that it is against the law to remove cultural and archeological resources on federal land."

"That could be the reason the owners of that suitcase don't want to be exposed," Josie said. "They found the ivory on federal land."

"Not to mention the elephant ivory which is definitely illegal," Dora said in disgust.

"But why would they risk breaking the law, if they could just buy the ivory from the Eskimos?"

"It's cheaper that way. Look what ivory sells for." Dora pointed to the print on the page. "A single ivory tusk sells in the thousands."

"Okay, it's worth money. Why did we find the suitcase en route to Alaska, instead of coming from Alaska?"

Dora shook her head. "Another question I can't answer." She slid her finger down the page and stopped to mull over a few more facts. "The woolly mammoth has thought to have been preserved from 10,000 to 400,000 years ago."

"Impressive, but I feel sad for the shaggy beasts," Josie said and then frowned. "And the poor elephants are on the verge of extinction."

"Remember, Josie, it wasn't our fault that the woolly mammoths disappeared. I suppose it had to do with climate change." She read further. "The ivory has to be dried out or it will deteriorate."

"Makes sense," Josie said. "Hard to imagine the tusks survived that long."

"Listen to this. Mammoth ivory ranges from creams to browns and occasionally green and blue. It depends on the minerals the ivory absorbed."

"Hard to believe it's not illegal to use it."

"It's estimated there are thousands of tons of ivory under the permafrost. Oh, wait." Dora held up her hand. "I see here that's it's illegal to ship and sell mammoth ivory in New Jersey, New York, and California."

"Why is that?"

"Seems the poachers pass the elephant ivory off as mammoth ivory."

"Good grief. Poor elephants killed for their ivory."

"Josie, I think that's what we have here, hence the mixture of elephant and mammoth ivory."

"We've really gotten ourselves into something big this time."

Dora continued to read. "Several countries are big purchasers of ivory. Tighter regulations might be imposed for the mammoth ivory, too."

"Reminds me of the buffalo nearly hunted to extinction because of their hides and tongues. Can you imagine killing an animal for its tongue? Have people no conscience?"

"And the eagle for its feathers, the whale for its oil and its ivory? The list goes on and on."

Josie slumped in her chair. "Interesting information, but we're no closer to solving who the ivory belongs to."

"You're right. Let's call it a night and head back to our cabins."

Josie put the books back where they found them and followed Dora to the elevator. "Shall we bunk together again for the night?"

"It's okay with me. Which cabin?"

"Let's check them both out," Josie suggested. "We'll start with mine." She inserted the key card into her lock when they arrived and entered cautiously. Dora stood right behind her and gasped nearly the same time as Josie let out a squeal. "They've hit my room, too."

"What a mess. They're still looking for the ivory." She noticed a large slip of paper on the bedside table and picked it up. Her hands shook. "Listen to this Josie. 'You have our ivory and we want it back. Leave it on the lido deck within the hour. We will be watching you.'"

"They know we have it," Josie said as she peeked under the bed. "Dora, the suitcase is gone."

"Yes, apparently they don't want to leave any evidence, but how did they know we had the suitcase?"

"Oh, Dora, this mystery is leading us in way too deep. We need the guys here or else we need to report this."

"I'm beginning to agree with you. If our men aren't coming soon, we must tell the authorities what we know."

"For sure they won't be here within the hour. And if we don't return the cache what will happen to us?"

Both sisters shook with fright after reading the threatening note. "What should we do?" Josie asked her sister apparently unable to think.

"We must tell the ship's security. But we can't leave this room for fear of being followed."

"How can anyone follow us? No one is ever in the hallway."

"Perhaps, they have installed a camera somewhere. Or maybe they are part of the crew and have access to security devices."

"Gosh never thought of that. So can we trust anyone?" Josie asked.

"I'm not sure. I'd better send Milton an S.O.S."

Not long after Dora texted a message to Milton explaining the situation and admitting she hadn't turned in the suitcase to the authorities as he had advised, he replied. "I'll be in Juneau tomorrow. Sit tight and don't leave the room until morning. Anthony will stay here and finish our assignment."

"He didn't yell at me," Dora said to Josie bewildered.

"Bet he will when he meets us in Juneau. I hope we're safe tonight."

Dora wrung her hands. "I'm sure we will be. Why would they harm us? We are the only ones who know where the ivory is."

Josie trembled. "That's just it. They could threaten to do us in unless we talk, and they must have the key to get in."

"That thought is scary," Dora admitted. "One of us has to keep watch while the other sleeps."

"Oh, Dora, our situation is just like the movies."

Dora and Josie didn't waste a moment as they piled up furniture against the cabin door and turned the dead bolt. "I volunteer for second watch," Dora said.

"But what do we do in the morning?" Josie wanted to know.

"We'll call for room service and then change our mind and accompany the waiter back to the main floor where we can blend in with people. Too bad, we couldn't disguise ourselves in some way."

"Sorry, I didn't pack my masquerade kit," Josie said dryly. "I'm going to try to sleep while you figure out what to do in the morning." Josie prepared herself for bed and in no time at all she was snoring lightly.

After selecting the heaviest object in the room to use as a weapon, Dora positioned herself in a chair next to the door, so she could hear if anyone dared to intrude. The hours slowly ticked away, and several times she caught herself dozing. Banging noises in the hall awakened her. Too afraid of going to the door to peek out, she remained rigid in her chair. Instead of waking Josie, Dora assumed the watch throughout the night.

————

Late morning, Otto sat at the bar alone, drinking Scotch. The bartender called him by his registered name and poured him another drink. He had boarded the ship under his given name, using the alias Otto only when he was out on the tundra. Otto racked his brain in confusion over the disappearance of his black suitcase and his last rash attempts to find it. His last caper turned up empty.

Sweat beads formed on Otto's forehead when he thought of the huge chance he took, breaking into one of the cabins aboard ship. He had determined that the cabin he had broken into was occupied by one female.

The worst part, Otto thought, was that the black suitcase was nowhere to be found in the cabin. He had torn the place apart and found nothing. So where was the suitcase? Did the woman give it to the authorities?

After conducting a few discreet inquiries, he had discovered the cabin in question was occupied by a couple, Dora and Milton and the next door cabin by her sister, Josie and Anthony

The other evening when the women were out, he made one more attempt to find the case and broke into the cabin next door. He had found the suitcase, but it was empty. Why would two women make off with his stash? Did they know its value? Baffled on what to do, and even though it was risky, he had written them a threatening note and taken the empty suitcase with him. Then he waited for them to come out. Surely, two lone women would cave to his demands.

He had waited all night and into the morning when he heard pounding on the door down the hall. Looking through the peephole, he saw a man knocking on their door. There was no way they would give in to his demands now. Men weren't so easily threatened. Deciding to come up with another ploy later, he climbed into bed for a few hours of sleep before he left his cabin.

Chapter Six

When evidence of daylight broke through the parted draped window, Dora let herself fall asleep until she heard Josie stir.

"Why didn't you wake me?"

Dora yawned. "No use both of us losing sleep."

"Apparently, you heard no one?"

"Nothing. I'm beginning to believe whoever wrote the note didn't intend to carry out the threat. Since we are two females, they probably thought we would come rushing out of the door with hands in the air. Ha, we fooled them."

Josie threw off the covers and scooted to the edge of the bed. "Since when did you become so brave?"

Dora smirked. "Since our first and second excursion. Don't you think we learned a thing or two about the criminal mind?"

"Now, you're exaggerating. Our husbands solved the crimes."

"But I believe it's safe to say we did pick up a few pointers."

"Alright, I admit we are a bit savvier than we used to be," Josie said. "Now let's get dressed and call room service, so we can get out of here."

"I get the shower first," Dora called.

"You win." Josie laughed. "After all, you did let me sleep."

Dora grabbed her robe from the closet. "Listen to my phone. Milton may be sending a message."

Josie nodded that she would.

While soaping her hair with the welcome warm water, Dora prayed she was making the right decisions. Josie had been very observant about her recent behavior. Why was she being so brave? After all, she was the one that had been afraid to leave home. Shrugging off the answer, she turned the water off, and stepped out of the shower. She heard Josie's panicked voice.

"Dora, someone is knocking on our door."

"Oh, my gosh," She shouted back. "Wait 'til I put on my robe." Her heart thumped wildly as she wiggled into her underclothes and robe. She opened the bathroom door to hear the knocking herself.

"Dora, let me in."

"It's…it's Milton," Dora shrieked. "Milton, is that you," she yelled back.

"Yes, Dora. Please let me in."

Dora raced to the door and pressed her face to the peephole to confirm his presence, and then unlocked the door and jerked it open.

His eyes held alarm. "Are you two alright?"

"We are. Come in," Dora said breathlessly. "I didn't expect you so soon." She locked the door after them.

"I was about ready to break the door down."

"You really were?" Josie asked wide-eyed.

"I came as soon as I could. I believe what you have told me is serious."

"We think so, too," Dora said as he encircled her in his arms. "I'm so glad to see you."

"Now tell me everything you know."

Dora sent Josie to the shower pouting while she filled Milton in on every detail she could remember. She handed him the note that was left in the room.

He held the note in his hand. "Did the threat put a scare into you?"

"I have to admit it did, but we didn't cave into their demands although I didn't sleep last night."

"I'm proud of you, but you should have turned the suitcase in as soon as you found it. You could have been in great danger."

She flinched. "Perhaps, but I wanted to do something to prove I have changed."

"I love you for who you are. You don't have to change and become someone you're not," he told her.

"You don't think I botched the situation?"

He hesitated. "No…no, I don't believe so."

"Where shall we begin, then?" she asked him.

"First of all we'll enjoy Juneau. I don't think there's any rush until I can snoop around a while."

"What about the ivory we have hidden?"

"Leave it where it is for now. I am anxious to see it, but it's best to see if we're being followed."

"I haven't told you everything about the cache. Last night we learned from one of our table partners that mammoth ivory is used as a cover for elephant ivory which is illegal. In that suitcase we found varying white shapes that look different from the raw mammoth ivory. I feel we are dealing with actual crooks."

"Sounds that way. This task might be something the federal authorities must handle."

"We won't get into trouble for not reporting it right-a-way?"

Milton ran his fingers through his cropped-red hair. "I'm not sure."

Dora immediately noticed the worry on Milton's face. What had she done? She had unintentionally interfered with federal law, maybe international law. She rose from the chair and grabbed her clothes from the closet not really cognizant of what she chose. "Are you going to talk to security?" Too modest to dress in front of him, she tossed the garments on the bed until the bathroom was unoccupied.

"I'll make a decision when Anthony comes aboard, but it seems the only recourse."

"Anthony's coming here soon?" Josie inquired, stepping out of the bathroom.

"You heard us?" Dora asked in surprise.

"I didn't take a shower, just freshened up a bit. I'm ready." She announced while adding earrings to complete her look.

"I left Anthony to pick up the loose ends as well as research mammoth ivory and other matters related," Milton explained. "He should be here at the next port-of-call."

"Oh, the cruise will be half over by then," Josie wailed.

"Have you noticed anyone follow you?" Milton asked.

Dora shook her head. "That's the strange part. We haven't noticed anyone unusual. But someone ransacked our cabins and left us a threatening note."

"Where is the empty black suitcase now?" Milton asked.

"In Josie's cabin," Dora said. "I was going to ditch it in the laundry room."

"I'd like to dust it for fingerprints before we do anything."

"Right now?" Josie asked.

Milton nodded. Josie led him to her cabin and covered her mouth to stifle a scream when she saw the room had been broken into. After a quick search, Josie held her hands up to her face and shrieked, "It's not here."

Milton examined the lock and shook his head.

Josie lost no time in running back to Dora's cabin to tell her that her room was broken into and the suitcase was missing.

"I don't believe the nerve of this individual. Was anything else taken?" Dora asked.

Milton shook his head. "Just the suitcase."

"What do we do now?" Dora slipped her hands into her jacket pocket.

"We must report it so the lock can be fixed," Milton said. "Let's make the most of our time and tour Juneau."

"You want to tour at a time like this?" Dora asked incredulously.

"Yes, at the moment I can do nothing. I don't want to reveal my career choice at this moment. It won't do any good to dust for prints. Whoever we are dealing with is too smart to leave prints."

Dora took a deep breath and attempted to calm herself. Guilt was taking over, but she realized Milton was right. What good would it do to remain in the cabin worrying.

"Keep your eyes open for familiar faces. What is it that you would like to see most?"

Josie raised her hand. "I'd like to see the Mendenhall Glacier."

Dora decided not to tell Josie the trouble they might be in for not reporting the mix-up with the suitcases. It was best to let her enjoy her day. After all, it was Dora's fault they were in this mess.

———

Milton and the sisters decided to tour Juneau on their own rather than pay for the cruise related tour. Juneau, the capital of Alaska, proved to be a delightful historic town with Native cultural influence. Dora and Josie marveled at the many cruise ships docked to explore the city. "It appears the tourists take over the town," Dora said.

They quickly learned that the only way to reach Juneau was by plane or boat since the rugged terrain surrounding the city prohibited a road network. "A little too isolated for me," Josie remarked, shivering. "The mountains certainly hem in the city."

Atop the rugged mountains the enormous Juneau ice field of thirty glaciers emerged, two visible from the local road system. Mendenhall Glacier was one which they chose to view.

They had discussed it might be appropriate to check out scrimshaw and ivory trinkets and jewelry in Juneau before they visited the glacier.

From shop owners, they learned that ivory in Alaska could be found and enjoyed in three forms. The Alaskan natives were exempted from restrictions on its use. The Alaskan natives still hunted fresh water walrus from skin boats, and they were the only ones who could collect and carve the bright white ivory. Ancient walrus ivory which could be blue, red, and black in color could also be used by non-whites as well as the mammoth ivory.

"Did you notice that fresh walrus ivory is white?" Dora asked a hint of optimism to her tone.

Milton tilted his head in thought. "So perhaps the white ivory you gals found is not elephant but walrus?"

Dora nodded and gritted her teeth.

Milton drew her next to him. "Don't worry. We'll find the answer. It will work out."

She prayed what he told her was true. Why had she gone and made a fool of herself by practically shedding tears to boot. Ordinarily, she didn't hang herself out on a limb like she did. Why did she feel the need to impress Milton? All she had accomplished was to look like a ninny. After all the years of being so careful not to appear foolish and vulnerable she just did. Emotion did that to a person. She had always know that.

Josie focused on the display cases. "Dora, are you going to buy a piece of ivory as a token of our trip?"

"I'm thinking something carved out of soapstone. I believe I have enough memory of ivory to last me a while."

Milton laughed. "Pick out something and I'll buy it for you."

Dora admired the Alaskan natives cast in everyday activities and carved from the green soapstone. The prices were more than she would pay, but since Milton offered to give her one as a gift, she chose the Eskimo wielding a harpoon. Milton smiled at her when the clerk rang up the purchase.

Josie scrutinized the scrimshaw jewelry but decided to wait for Anthony before making a selection. "If I'm spending this much money on myself, I want Anthony's input," she told her sister. "I wonder if Ted and Alicia are shopping for ivory."

"They probably are, but there are a lot of shops to choose from." Dora looked up and down the street when they left the shop.

Considering they had more ports-of-call ahead of them which included shopping, they decided to take the shuttle from the city to the glacier. A stop at the visitor center, resting on a bluff was a must. As they approached it, Josie remarked that the building's center portion resembled a flying saucer.

"Have you ever seen one," Dora asked in humor. The excursion as well as Milton's encouragement had taken her mind off her blunders.

"Well no, but that's how they're depicted."

One inside, they discovered the many windows reaching out to the beauty surrounding them. From many vantage points the thirteen-mile glacier dominated center stage with its transparent lake at the base. The roar of Nugget Falls added to the excitement as it cascaded down the mountain near the glacier.

Hiking trails enabled them to walk near the lake and to marvel at the mass of frozen ice butted up against the water. The glacier posed as if suspended in a frozen time warp.

When they had enough of hiking, they returned to the trolley. Josie's face glowed pink with the outdoor excursion. "Oh, that was fun. My quilt pattern does seem similar to a glacier. Every time I work with it, I'll think of the real one I just saw."

"You'll see several more before we conclude the trip," Dora said wryly. "You must have taken at least two dozen photos of it."

"The view was beautiful, not that any picture can capture how breathtaking the glacier is, but I tried. The white frozen ice seemed to flow into the serene lake below it. Didn't you think?" Josie made a surging motion with her hands. "How can one not get excited by such a natural display?"

"I agree," Milton concluded. "Dora has become too distracted searching for familiar faces."

Josie scrolled through the photos she took, showing several of her favorites to Milton and Dora. "So have you noticed anyone familiar, Dora?"

"As a matter-of-fact I did."

Josie dropped the phone camera to her side. "Really? Who?"

"I saw Alicia and Ted."

Josie frowned. "You did? Wish you would have told me."

"Sorry. I didn't know they're important to you."

"I'd like to have found out if Alicia bought anything. She's planning a quilt wall hanging of woolly mammoths to hang in her museum."

"Ambitious project. I assume she can draw well?" Dora said.

"She's quite talented."

Dora linked her arm in Milton's. "You'll meet them at dinner tonight. They're our table partners, and they know a lot about ivory and Alaskan culture."

Milton's eyes lit up. "They do?"

"Now don't get any ideas." Dora frowned. "They're good people. Own a museum. Besides, they would be too obvious to be the culprits."

"I look forward to meeting them," Milton said with adventure clouding his voice. "I suppose it's highly unlikely with thousands aboard ship that they would be the guilty ones."

Dora didn't like the sound of his tone. She knew him well enough that he didn't always share what he was thinking. He was a good detective, and if anyone could find the crooks it would be Milton. She vowed to stay out of his way and let him work, but she felt terrible she had gotten them all in this predicament by not turning the suitcase in immediately.

Once Dora and Milton were alone in their cabin dressing for dinner, Milton let down his reserve and admitted to Dora how he had missed her. He caught her in his arms and nibbled on her ear. She gently pushed him away with a "Not now, Milton."

He realized she was preoccupied with her gaffe. Even though she continually expressed regret for being so careless with the uninvited suitcase, he assured her with hugs and ardent kisses that he would make things right. And to smooth over the situation, he opened his suitcase and handed her a large bag. Dora narrowed her eyes at his gift, but she opened it at his command and lifted out a glittering red evening dress.

"Red? Milton. What were you thinking?"

Milton swallowed the hurt rising in his throat. "Don't you like it?" He took the dress and held it up to her.

"Well, the thought is just beautiful. I...I love you for it. But red! It's so showy. And sparkly."

"I think you'll look divine. Put it on," he said, his voice cracking a bit.

As usual Dora disappeared into the bathroom and remained there a while. "Dora, are you okay?" Milton called while scratching the back of his neck.

"I...don't think this dress is for me."

"Why not?"

"It's kind of tight and a little too low cut."

Milton felt his blood rush with anticipation. "Come out, Dora. I'm your husband. You shouldn't be embarrassed."

Slowly the door creaked open and Dora emerged slowly. Her face almost matched the color of her dress. Milton thought she looked beautiful and to him the dress fit perfectly. It wasn't too tight as his wife had told him. And low cut? He didn't think so. He chuckled inwardly thinking she had been so modest all her life that an expanse of exposed skin alarmed her.

"Are you ready?" He asked offering his arm.

Her mouth gaped. "You mean for me to wear this in public?"

"Of course. You're beautiful." He bent and kissed her lips, tenderly.

Dora blushed. "What will Josie think?"

"She'll think the same as I do."

Dora fidgeted with the length, muttering about the hem. "I believe I should ask her opinion before we leave."

Milton shrugged and let her depart the cabin to knock on Josie's door. He heard approving sounds from Josie and smiled to himself for winning Josie's consent. Peeking out the door, he witnessed Josie circling Dora and admiring her from every angle. He stepped out and checked his watch. "Ladies I'm ready to escort you both to dinner."

"Well, I just don't know—"

"There's no time to change," Milton told Dora brusquely.

"You look wonderful. For the first time you outshine me," Josie said unabashed as she smoothed her lime green lace tunic and skirt.

Dora grimaced. "And that's supposed to comfort me." She looked to Milton to save her, but he only smiled. "We look like the Christmas duo."

Just before they entered the dining room, Dora stopped and turned toward Milton. "I don't think we should tell everyone you're a detective."

"Anyone can find out who I really am with an online search."

"That maybe true, but let's let them work at it."

"Have you always been a detective?" Josie asked.

"I've worked construction when I was young."

"Okay," Dora said. "We'll say you're a retired construction worker."

Milton nodded. "If you wish." He formed a scenario in his mind and hoped he could get through the conversation without blowing his cover.

Josie frowned. "Milton, a construction worker? He's too sophisticated, and his hands are too soft."

Milton noticed the stares directed toward Dora when they arrived at the dining room. He smiled to himself for choosing the right gift. She fit in perfectly with the other women who were dressed to the nines. Why she hid her beauty the way she did puzzled him. And the glow she now possessed had something to do with him, he was sure.

After introductions were made and pleasantries exchanged, Milton skillfully guided the conversation from him to other matters. More often, he sat and listened to the couples around him, paying special attention to Alicia and Ted.

Milton noticed Dora attempted to guide the discussion to ivory and scrimshaw, but tonight no one seemed to be interested. Ted and Alicia didn't bite on Dora's proposed topic. Janelle and Don dominated the discussion with their whale watching adventure. The retired couple Bridgett and Bill said they had toured Juneau on their own.

Milton had prided himself on sizing up people, but his impression of the table guests weren't firm in his mind. Perhaps another meal with them would yield more.

Once alone, Dora asked him his impressions of the diners. Milton shook his head. "Sorry, I have nothing for you. Too soon to make an assessment."

After dinner, Milton invited the sisters to locate a lounge for dancing. "I'm just too distraught with the situation to dance." Dora waved away the idea.

"But I want to show you off," Milton said. "We're here to enjoy the cruise not to worry about some missing ivory."

She tossed him a glance of frustration. "How can you be so noncommittal?"

He shrugged. "Why ruin a perfectly good evening."

Josie stared at Dora and frowned. "Now if Anthony were here, I'd jump at the chance." She latched onto Dora's arm and dragged her along.

Milton smiled at his accomplice.

Dora broke free of their restraints. "Alright then. Just don't keep me out too long. We're sewing tomorrow."

Milton took turns dancing with the sisters to soft piano music of "Blue Moon." At first, Dora was tense and stiff but eventually settled into his arms. He had to admit to himself that she was challenging at times, but he had no doubt she was a caring woman. When he changed partners and asked Josie to dance, she pointed out Janelle and Don who were on the side-line listening to the music. "What do you know about that couple?" Milton asked Josie.

"Not much other than they are seasoned travelers and this is their fourth cruise."

"Is she in your quilting class?'

"She is. She's going to be doing the glacier star. It's very complicated. More for the experienced quilter. I doubt she'll get it done before the cruise concludes."

"Bridgett isn't in your classes?"

"No, I haven't seen her."

"Strange Janelle would sign up for a quilting cruise. They could afford to go anywhere. Why this cruise?" Milton mused.

———

Since they had slept in after a late night out, Dora and Josie offered Milton a rain check on breakfast the following morning. Dora mumbled to Josie her consternation with Milton for keeping her out after midnight.

Josie sighed. "Will you ever change?"

Dora ignored her as usual and once inside the sewing room, both she and Josie approached the compartments to retrieve their sewing projects. Both gasped about the same time, when they immediately noticed Dora's key was unnecessary. The lock had been broken. The sisters whispered frantically between themselves when they discovered the stash of ivory was gone from Dora's sewing compartment. Josie's cubicle was still secure, and the bundle was safety hidden inside.

"I should immediately tell Milton," Dora whispered to Josie.

"I don't believe it's a good idea to arouse suspicion. Better to wait. What can he do now, anyway?"

"Do you honestly think the perpetrator is in the sewing room?"

Josie shrugged. "Or knows someone in this sewing room."

Dora held the quilt pieces in her hand. "We had better move the cache from your compartment before we leave this room."

"Right now?"

"Yes, now. I'll shield you with my quilt backing." Dora opened up the plain back and pretended to inspect the fabric.

Josie grasped the bundle from her locker and dropped it into her bag.

"Josie, your face is all red. You look like you just committed a major crime."

"I can't help it. I feel we're mixed up in some awful scheme. First we have the cache and then we don't. Someone is playing a game with us."

"I hope it isn't a dangerous one. Just hang on to the cache until we can meet with Milton."

"How do you think they found your stash and why didn't they break my lock, too. By now, the perpetrators should know we're connected."

"I have no idea, but we'd better split before we draw attention to ourselves."

Josie crowded in next to the locker. "Too late now, here comes your New York sewing neighbor, Briana."

Dora cringed, closed the door, and backed up against the lockers, managing a grin.

Briana laughed. "You ladies looked as if you swallowed a fly. Anything I can help you with?"

Dora choked out a response. "No, No. Just a late night, I guess. Having trouble getting organized."

Briana smirked. "Oh, I see. Newlyweds. How cute." With a disdainful look, she turned and glided toward her machine.

Josie frowned. "What was that all about?"

"Have no idea."

Dora rethought her sudden outburst of fright, took out her sewing project and hoped no one would notice that the lock had been broken. Doing her best to calm herself with deep breaths, she proceeded to her sewing machine to await directions from her instructor.

"Hope we see Milton at lunch," Dora said as a parting comment.

Dora truly hoped she would, so she could give Milton what was left of the ivory. She had confidence he would know what to do. Briana had just called the instructor over for assistance when Dora sat down and searched for the appliqué pieces in her kit. Today she would be working on an appliqué for her northern lights quilt. Her squares of pastels were almost sewn together leaving room for an appliqué of an Eskimo fishing. By the time she sewed all the squares together the quilt would have room for two appliqués. She considered a cabin and a moose. As she laid out the pieces on her squares, she glanced over to Briana's project, noticing her squares depicting the northern lights were not aligned as expertly as an accomplished quilter would although Dora reminded herself the classes were open to all levels of quilters. Why was she being so critical?

Luckily, Briana absorbed herself in the quilt and kept the personal questions at bay. Dora sighed in relief. She didn't appreciate Briana probing into her life. Just because they were sitting together didn't entitle her to become a bosom buddy, Dora thought. Ashamed of her current feelings, she thought back to Christmas and to her changed attitude, but this was different. Briana was annoying, but that didn't mean she couldn't be kind.

Dora's sewing machine had hummed for an hour, when the instructor came over to her table and called her aside. Panic crept into Dora's throat. Had something happened to Milton?

"I noticed your lock has been broken," the instructor began. "Why didn't you say something?"

"Oh that," Dora said attempting to make light of the incident. "I guess someone wanted my project." She attempted a chuckle.

The instructor facial expression of concern didn't change. "Was anything taken?"

"Oh, no. That's why I didn't say anything."

"Do you want to file a complaint?"

Dora shook her head. "Not necessary."

"Very well then, but if you change your mind please let me know. I'll assign you to a new locker. Want me to help you move the contents?"

"Oh, no," Dora said too forcefully. There really isn't anything left. Ah, I mean there's nothing left to worry about."

"What was that about?" Briana wanted to know after the instructor left.

"Nothing," Dora said flatly and continued with her appliqué.

"I overheard you're going to be given a new locker. Was there something wrong with the one you have now?"

"Just the lock. It's not working properly."

"Oh, I see."

Relieved that Briana returned to her quilt, she hoped the teacher would not tell the class what had happened to her locker.

Dora watched the clock as she was anxious to meet with Milton for lunch. Just as she feared, the instructor warned the quilters to lock up their projects, announcing that one locker had been broken into. Luckily, she didn't announce the name, but Briana looked at her and smiled. "Why didn't you tell me?"

Dora couldn't wait to speak to Milton. Briana hinted about joining her for lunch to learn the details of the broken lock, but Dora brushed her off with an explanation of a prior engagement. As soon as the quilters were dismissed, Dora dashed out the door and joined Josie. "Do you have the cache," Dora whispered, peering over her shoulder.

"I do, but I can't wait to get rid of it. Having it in my possession makes me very uneasy."

The sisters spotted Milton at the salad bar. They assumed the line behind him and said nothing until they were seated with their lunch. "Milton, I have something frightening to tell you," Dora said as casually as she could. "Shall I tell you here or wait?"

"Tell me now just as if we were having a normal conversation."

She swallowed. "The lock to my storage compartment was broken and the stash was taken."

"Before I even had a look at it? I should have investigated right away," Milton frowned.

"But I still have my cache," Josie broke in. "For some reason they didn't break my lock."

"The perpetrators were probably scared away," Milton surmised with an aura of experience. "Do you have the goods with you?"

"I do, and I wish you'd take them."

"We can't transfer them here. Someone could be watching."

"So what do I do?" Josie demanded.

"We'll make the exchange after we leave the dining area. Some place no one is watching."

"And where is that?"

"Our cabin. No cameras there."

Milton and the ladies finished eating their meal as casually as possible although Dora found it difficult to swallow any food. Her stomach was flip-flopping, and her heart hammered in her chest. When they had finished, Milton told them to follow him and walk fast when they were clear of the main area. He led them at a speedy clip until they reached Milton's cabin. As soon as they were inside the cabin, Josie pulled the bag out of her purse and handed it to Milton. "After your sewing class, come back directly to the cabin," he told the sisters. "I may have a plan by then."

Chapter Seven

"I spoke to Anthony," Milton told Dora and Josie when they returned from their sewing class early in the afternoon.

Josie kicked off her shoes and nestled into a chair. "What did he have to say?"

"Anthony's intensely studying the ivory trade. He'll tell us what he found out when he joins the cruise tomorrow."

Dora planted a kiss on Milton's forehead and settled on the edge of the bed. "Did Anthony give you any hints?"

"I studied the contents of the bag and emailed photos of it to Anthony. I'm no expert on ivory, but I see we have a mix of specimens. Some appears fossilized and other is white and pure."

"We noticed that, too," Dora said. "Can you guess at what it could be?"

"Anthony emailed me that some of it appears to be in raw form, the white pieces are called blanks. They're ready for scrimshaw art."

"Why is this loot en route to Alaska rather than coming from Alaska?" Josie asked. "Doesn't make sense to me."

"I believe it was to be given to someone aboard the cruise."

"You said you would have a plan?" Dora reminded him.

"I've enacted part of it." He ran his fingers through his cropped red hair. "I've had a talk with security, showed them my credentials. The ivory is now locked up in the ships safe."

"Good," Dora said in relief.

"Did Anthony agree with your plan?" Josie inquired while worry lines etched across her face.

"He did. With what I told him and what he has researched we thought it the right thing to do."

"So, it is serious?" Dora asked.

"It could be."

Josie rose from the chair to look out the window at the water. "I'm glad we're not involved any longer."

Milton rolled up his shirt sleeves and stretched. "Ah, but I am."

Dora moaned. "Milton, tell me you're not on this case."

"Sorry, Dora, but I couldn't tell the ship's security staff no."

Dora sighed in hopes Milton wouldn't read her true feelings. She had hoped for a romantic cruise with him, but now he would be involved in a case which might prove to be dangerous. Distracting him with frivolities would not be an option for her. Ah, well, she had her sewing and sight-seeing. The two activities would have to be enough for now. Josie's expression revealed the same conclusion about her and Anthony, she thought.

"We're done with sewing for today. The instructor released us early to enjoy the inland passage with the glaciers and gorgeous scenery," Dora said solemnly. "That is if you have time."

"Ah Dora, don't be upset." Milton smiled. "Of course I have time. Too bad Anthony will have to miss it, though."

Josie frowned and turned from the window. "I wish Anthony was here, but I'll do my best to have fun. Bring your coats and your best camera. I'm anticipating some rare photo opportunities."

Milton offered Dora a conciliatory gesture with a squeeze and a peck on the cheek which brought a little pink to her face. "What are we about to see, Milton?"

"Scenery. Some of the most beautiful on earth. And glaciers, of course."

"I love glaciers," Josie said. "An inspiration for my quilt."

"The Hubbard glacier is six-miles wide not to mention the magnificent fiords that were carved by glaciers."

"And why is it called the Inside Passage?" Dora asked.

"The Inside passage is an ocean route for sea-faring vessels that weaves its way through a network of islands on the Pacific coast."

Dora shivered and put on her jacket, expecting the deck to be quit chilly. The mention of glaciers didn't help any. They vied with passengers for a good view of the frozen mountains of ice. The ship came closer to the gleaming wall of ice than Dora had expected. A loud boom and crack caused her to jump and animated the other passengers as well. A roar of delight and surprise went up from the spectators as a chunk of ice broke off from the main glacier and plunged head long into water, making a dreadful booming noise. Janelle and Don, who were near, moved over toward them. "I just love to see the glaciers calving," Don told them, swiping the blond hair off his forehead.

Josie narrowed her eyes. "Calving?"

Janelle laughed. "The glacier calves or breaks out icebergs up to three and four stories high."

"Wow, I hope we don't run into one and sink," Josie said in alarm.

Milton lifted his brow. "Trust the Captain. He knows what he is doing."

Dora and Josie exchanged glances not sure if they should believe what Milton had just said.

"We've been here several times before and so far the ship has not sunk," Don said with a grin.

Josie smiled. "You have?"

"Oh, yes, the Inside Passage is one of our favorite places."

Not long after the heart-stopping jolt of calving, forest clad islands came into view, teeming with wildlife. Spectators took advantage of the scene, zeroing in with cameras on sea lions, porpoises, and even brown bears.

"Watch for whales," Milton said. "An orca whale sighting would surely top the day."

"Oh, yes, we have seen them on our travels," Don said. "They are magnificent."

"You have traveled a lot?" Milton asked.

Don nodded.

"What's your favorite place?"

Don paused. "Hard to say. I suppose the North Country."

Milton wondered why Don and Janelle returned to a place they had been several times before. Was there something else that drew them to Alaska?

———

That evening Milton clapped his hands for attention. "Ladies, how about a good meal with our dining companions? Perhaps they'll be more talkative tonight."

"I'm not wearing the red dress," Dora quickly said, expressing her show of authority.

Milton tapped his heart with his hand. "Dora, I'm hurt. I went to a lot of trouble to buy it for you."

"I appreciate your intentions. If I add a cape or a shrug I might be persuaded to wear it again." She smiled weakly. "I think a jacket would be better. Then it'd cover my hips."

"You're thin, Dora, you have no hips. But if it makes you feel better, it's a deal," he said, winking at her.

Feeling deflated after finding out the cruise would be a working cruise for the guys, both sisters opted for street-length dresses for the evening; neither had the desire to dress-up in all the finery. Dora suggested that Josie wear her gold dress, but she had planned to save it for Anthony. "It's picture night tomorrow evening," she reminded them.

Milton's eyes gleamed with an idea.

"Oh, no, you're thinking of the red dress," Dora murmured.

They arrived at their table before Alicia and Ted. Milton drew the chairs out for Josie and then Dora and settled in beside her. "I want to see what Alicia knows about ivory," he whispered to Dora.

"I believe she knows a lot. Good luck."

The mundane talk around the table repressed his hope for anything consequential until Alicia and Ted arrived late. She apologized for their tardy appearance, explaining that they had taken a late nap and almost overslept. "I wouldn't want to miss one of these scrumptious meals," Alicia said laughingly.

After they all had settled into their first course and conversation dwindled, Milton approached the subject of ivory, inquiring of Alicia if she had any advice on buying a scrimshaw piece at their next port-of-call. "Dora has told me you operate a museum and know of such things."

"Ted and I are familiar with the art of scrimshaw. What is it you want to know?" Alicia set down her fork and blotted her lips. Tron instantly was at her side and whisked her salad plate away along with a few others.

"I would like to purchase a fine piece, but am concerned if I'm buying the real thing. Can one tell if a piece of ivory is genuine?"

"Someone with experience and training will be able to, but I'm confident that if you choose a reputable store you will be fine."

Milton groaned inwardly as he wanted her to expose her knowledge, but she seemed to hedge at offering more. He then took the direct approach. "Are you able to tell the difference?"

"The difference?"

"Yes. Let's say between mammoth ivory and elephant ivory. I would assume they would appear the same since they are of the same species."

"The use of elephant ivory is illegal," she said curtly and directed her attention to the next course Tron was setting before her. She turned away from Milton and offered no more comments on ivory.

Accepting the rebuff as temporary, Milton turned his attention to the other couples, engaging them in a light conversation. Interested if Janelle and Don knew anything about ivory, he questioned them. To his surprise, they both knew quite a lot about ivory since they enjoyed visiting the North Country, admitting they had even made an excursion to the North Pole. He wanted to ask them if they had seen Santa but thought better of it.

Bridgett and Bill presented a challenge. Bridgett appeared difficult to please and often complained to Tron about the meal, sending Tron scurrying with one of her plates and returning from the kitchen with something more to her liking. Milton noticed Tron hovered over her as if she was the only diner at the table. Husband Bill paid no attention to his wife but huddled over his meal like a lion over a kill. Milton gave up on striking up any conversation with the two; instead, focusing on Dora.

"What shall we do after dining, my dear?" He asked. "A walk on the deck?"

"I think it rather chilly."

"I'd keep you warm," he whispered to her.

She felt his warm breath on her neck. "I know you would, but I don't want to leave Josie alone. Somehow, I don't sense we are completely safe," she whispered in his ear.

———

Desiring an early morning start, the sisters and Milton avoided the sit-down breakfast in the dining room. Instead, they crowded in line with the cruise passengers at the breakfast bars in anticipation of a day of sight-seeing in Skagway, the gateway to the Klondike gold rush of 1898. Anthony had contacted them he would be boarding the ship in Skagway in the late afternoon. Because of his late arrival, they had chosen a tour by the White Pass and Yukon Route Railway train which would take part of the day. Josie lamented that Anthony would miss Alaska's gold rush history. Milton advised her to take plenty of pictures.

After the ship's photographer shoot of the three disembarking from the ship, a short walk from the ship brought them to vintage nineteenth century carriages in which they would ride to the train. Once aboard, a guide began with the rich history of the Klondike gold rush, explaining the train would take them about twenty miles to the summit of White Pass. On this tour, he explained that they would see glaciers, mountains, waterfalls, tunnels, trestles, and historic sites of the gold rush. The scenery proved to be as every bit as splendid as the guide promised, providing many opportunities for photos although there weren't hardly any stops for a short hike. Dora didn't mind not walking, but she noticed Milton seemed antsy. She, however, was content to sit any enjoy the view from the train.

"Anyone here on this train you gals recognize," Milton asked.

"Just Bridgett," Dora answered. "I wonder where Bill is."

Josie snickered. "He seems to me to be bored with this cruise."

"Yes, I saw her, too," Milton added.

"Then why did you ask?" Dora said with a frown.

"Just to see if you were paying attention like I asked."

"Trying to make detectives from us, too?" Josie giggled.

"I actually was in favor of the zip-lining," Milton said, smiling directly at Dora who was becoming a bit miffed at her husband.

"We could have gone our separate ways," Dora suggested with a scowl.

"And leave you gals alone? No, never."

Dora's tone softened. "Are you saying that we need protection?"

"It's best to be vigilant," Milton said grimly.

Even though the tour was informative, Dora could sense that Anthony's arrival was on everyone's mind; however, the fully narrated tour interrupted thoughts and discussion among them about what Anthony may have discovered. It was probably for the best, Dora thought.

When they returned to Skagway, there was still time to explore the town. "Shall we take a look at the scrimshaw like you said you would?" Josie asked Milton in jest. "Alicia might ask if you found anything."

"We could. Any objections?"

The sisters shrugged. "Lead the way," Josie urged him.

After a quick survey of the town, Milton pointed to a museum which advertised examples of Alaskan ivory. Outside the entrance, Josie spotted a totem pole and talked Dora and Milton to pose in front of it for a picture. Milton ignored Dora's pout and encircled her with his arm. "Smile Dora," Josie ordered through her cheesy smile.

The first thing they saw when they entered the rustic museum was a 30,000 year old mammoth tusk carved with scenes of Eskimos hunting mammoths. The scrimshaw carved on the walrus tusk were numerous and interesting. They learned that only the indigenous peoples could carve walrus tusks since it had been a lasting part of their tradition. Displays of the Russian occupation and the history of the Gold Rush period were also included in the museum. Beautiful baleen baskets made by Native Americans drew their attention to their craftsmanship.

After touring the museum, Josie coaxed them to the gift shop where ivory jewelry and scrimshaw were available for sale. Dora noticed that the ivory items for sale proudly displayed were Alaskan crafted.

Milton advised the sisters that if they wanted something ivory, Skagway might be a good place to purchase a souvenir. Dora and Josie had already discussed it between themselves and reached the conclusion that ivory had become a bad memory.

"How about a baleen basket made by the Alaskan Natives, then?" Milton asked Dora. "Only Alaska Natives are allowed to harvest and use baleen."

Dora moved over to the baskets made from flexible material from the mouth of baleen whales, thinking they would be expensive. The saleslady explained that the baleen baskets were difficult to construct and few were made, explaining that the baleen was cut in strips, soaked in water, attached to ivory disks and then coiled much like a reed basket. A carved ivory finial, often resembling an animal, topped off the basket's lid. Usually men did the weaving. Dora admitted she liked them and conceded she didn't mind the ivory handle. As she was making a decision about whether to purchase one, she glanced up to see Bridgett approaching the display. She nodded a greeting toward Dora and listened to the sales person's pitch.

The clerk, who seemed very interested in making a sale, further added that indigenous people used the baleen for mundane necessities such as cups, buckets, and sleds. "You may have remembered that the Victorians used baleen for corset stays, fishing rods, and even umbrella ribs."

Josie beamed. "Oh, sure. I remember seeing the corset stays in museums. Glad we didn't have to wear them."

The clerk smiled. "However, by 1920 whaling declined. Baleen baskets became an art form around 1918 as well as a source of income for basket makers." Dora noticed that the baskets were not only beautiful but too expensive for her budget.

Bridgett listened to the explanation on basket making and wrinkled her nose when she learned the weaving material came from the whale's mouth. She touched the material lightly with her finger and the clerk saw an opportunity for a sale. After sharing more information why a purchase would be a good investment, Bridgett said she'd pass on a basket. The clerk nodded in defeat.

Dora thanked the saleslady for taking time to explain the art of basket making and told her she would give the decision to purchase one some serious thought. The clerk accepted Dora's decision graciously and left them to their browsing.

Dora then turned to Bridgett and initiated light conversation by asking her if she enjoyed her train trip. Expecting a positive response, she was surprised when Bridgett broke into a tirade of complaints. As soon as Bridgett paused for a breath, Dora asked about Bill, inquiring if he was feeling ill.

"No, he doesn't especially enjoy tours."

Sighing deeply, Dora suggested to her companions that they continue on and visit a few more shops before meeting Anthony. Just as they exited the entrance to the shop, a man resembling Tron scooted past them. Josie turned abruptly for another look. "Wasn't that Tron?" she said to Dora.

"I thought it looked like him, too, but wouldn't he be at the ship working?"

———

Josie wasn't able to concentrate on shopping for souvenirs. Anthony dominated her thoughts. She had missed him and was troubled that the romantic cruise she had envisioned was turning out to be anything but. She hoped that Anthony and Milton could arrive at a conclusion to this baffling case and enjoy the few days they had left.

Instead of ivory or baleen baskets, Dora picked up resin figures of Eskimos, sled dogs, and totem poles, informing Josie she would display them all on a shelf in the living room. Josie thought it a fine idea and chose a few figures to purchase, too. "I can't get back to Iowa without something from Alaska," she told Dora.

After the fourth shop, Josie lost all interest in shopping. Butterflies consumed her stomach, and she nearly jumped out of her skin when her phone rang. She answered with bated breath. "It's Anthony," she squealed to the group. "We're to meet him at the dock." She all but ran to the designated location where a number of passengers were beginning to congregate. As soon as she saw him, she ran to his open arms. Milton and Dora kept a respective distance until they had greeted one another sufficiently. Josie wiped the tears from her face when Milton and Dora walked up to them.

"So good to see you ole pal," Milton said as he firmly shook Anthony's hand. "I'm depending on you for information on this ivory gambit we've stumbled into," he whispered.

"I do, but we need to be somewhere no one will hear or see us in deep conversation."

Josie's eyes grew round. "Should we be concerned?"

"I don't mean to scare you, but we could be involved with some bad people."

Josie wrapped her arm around his. "Like who?"

"Like I said, we need to be somewhere alone."

"Our cabins would be the best place," Milton suggested. "Besides, we need to freshen up before dinner. You will meet our dining companions, then."

"Are they special?"

"You will think so," Milton bated him.

"Lead the way," Anthony said, smiling at Josie.

After returning to the ship, Milton unlocked the door to their cabin and ushered them all in before he checked the hallway for anyone lingering. Seeing no one suspicious other than the staff about their duties, he closed the door. All eyes turned to Anthony.

"What?" he asked, turning out his palms and hunching his shoulders.

"Answers," Josie giggled.

"Who are the bad people?" Dora frowned.

He dropped into the nearest chair. "I can't be sure with whom we are dealing, but I do know that certain terrorists have sold elephant ivory to China for money to fund their nefarious schemes. I've been told as many as 30,000 elephants have been annihilated annually for their ivory."

"I had no idea," Josie whispered. "What a waste. Poor animals."

"Of course, dealing in illegal elephant ivory is a serious business, and I understand some countries are working to put a stop to the trading. Does some stash contain elephant ivory?"

"We don't really know. No one has identified anything," Milton began. "One bag has been stolen back and the other is locked in the ship's safe."

"So we should be talking with the ship's authorities?"

"Yes, they were going to give the contents to an expert to examine. We will meet with them around eight tonight."

"I'd rather someone else take charge of this case," Anthony expressed concern. "It might be something for the federal authorities."

"We'll decide tonight," Milton cautioned.

"Suppose none of the contents contain elephant ivory, then who are we dealing with?" Dora asked.

"Good question," Milton said. "That's what we must find out."

"Either way, I wish we wouldn't have been delivered the wrong suitcase," Josie complained.

Anthony scratched his head. "I'm wondering how the suitcase passed inspection in the first place?"

"And if the package stolen back contained elephant ivory?" Milton added.

Chapter Eight

After dining with the couples, Milton asked Anthony his first impression of their dinner companions as they left the room.

"I'd like to get to know them better, but I would say Janelle and Don have been many places, but they are hesitant to share their experiences. They lead a free lifestyle by the way they dress. Ted and Alicia know more than they let on."

"They've been to China," Milton reminded him.

"That doesn't mean they're furnishing China ivory."

"No, but interesting."

"Bridgett and Bill seem like a miserable couple."

Milton laughed. "Miserable?"

"A nagging wife isn't miserable?"

"What about Tron?" Milton added with a grin.

"The waiter?" Anthony shrugged. "He seems competent and pays special attention to demanding Bridgett."

"Strange you would pick up the same impression as I have," Milton said. "I was hoping you would have more although I thought I detected a hint of familiarity between Bridgett and Tron."

Anthony furrowed his brow. "So you think they know one another?"

Milton shrugged. "Just a thought."

"They could have met him on another cruise," Josie said.

"Possibly," Milton said unconvinced.

Anthony turned to Josie. "Do we have time for dancing before we meet with the ship's security team?"

"I believe you deserve a few turns around the dance floor," Milton granted. "Dora, do you want to join them?"

"If you want. I'm not much of a dancer."

"I believe we should blend in with the crowd. We could learn something."

Several dancing venues aboard ship appealed to them, but in the end they chose a piano bar with a dance floor. The music was dreamy and evoked a sense of relaxation. Anthony and Josie danced each number while Milton and Dora danced a few and then sat out the rest.

Milton reached for Dora's hand. "There are so many people aboard ship that I fear we will never find out who brought the black suitcase aboard."

"Milton, you should be relaxing and not dwelling on the suitcase."

"I know." He patted her hand. "An unsolved case disturbs me. Both Anthony and I are sorry that your cruise hasn't turned out the way you planned."

Dora forced a smile. "We've been through disappointment before and have survived. Don't worry."

"Thanks for understanding." He kissed her cheek. "Do you recognize anyone here?"

Dora nodded toward the dance floor. "The willowy lady in the glitzy silver dress is my sewing neighbor. She's from New York and drives me crazy with chatter."

He chuckled at her comment. "Does she get much quilting done?"

"Not really. I have the feeling she's not really into quilting and shouldn't be there." Dora squinted at the dance floor. "Wait a minute. She's dancing with our waiter, Tron."

"You're right. It's odd that Tron works as a waiter, but we see him fraternizing with the passengers. I had better check him out in addition to your sewing partner. What's her name?"

"Briana. Guess I don't know her last name. I'll see if I can get it for you."

"Thanks. I'd appreciate it."

"Does she have a husband?"

"I don't know. Never asked."

"I suggest you start paying attention to what she has to say."

Dora stiffened at the suggestion. "I doubt if she's a suspect. There are thousands on this ship. It could be any one of them. How do you expect to find the culprit?"

"We'll have to do a check on everyone."

"Wouldn't it be likely that whoever brought the ivory aboard left the ship in Skagway?"

"I've thought of that possibly, but I hope they're still around, waiting for the opportunity to get back the other part of their ivory cache that we have locked in the safe."

"I think it would make more sense for the supposed thieves to leave before they are caught."

Milton glanced at his watch. "Time to go. Hate to break up the love birds but duty calls."

When Milton caught Anthony's attention he pointed to his watch. Anthony nodded that he understood and escorted Josie from the dance floor. They walked to the cabin where the men left the ladies for the night. "I think it best you stay in the cabins when we're not near," Milton cautioned. Dora and Josie looked at each other in alarm but agreed without comment.

Two men were waiting for Milton and Anthony in the Captain's office. Milton didn't recognize either one. After introductions, a young man by the name of Jack opened the discussion informing Milton and Anthony that an expert in Skagway examined the ivory and had determined there was a piece of elephant ivory among walrus ivory and the mammoth ivory. He explained that walrus ivory was possibly illegal, too, since only the Native people could acquire and use it. Jack also told them that they would assume the investigation but would appreciate any leads or help that Milton and Anthony could give them.

"Have you discovered anything helpful?" Jack swiped blonde hair out of his eyes.

"With this many people on board, it's difficult to focus on a suspect," Milton explained. "Are we able to do background checks on some passengers, the ones without families for example."

"Certainly. We'll get to it immediately. Would you like to help?"

Milton and Anthony exchanged glances. "The girls will be sewing tomorrow," Anthony told Milton.

"We'll help tomorrow," Milton offered. After more discussion concerning the logistics of background checks, the men returned to their cabins. "Let's not tell the ladies what we will be doing tomorrow. Let them think we aren't involved in this case," Anthony suggested.

"Good idea. They don't need to worry anymore."

———

Sewing classes resumed the next morning. Dora vowed she would listen to Briana chatter and try to glean something of importance. Milton had told her he intended to sun himself on deck while enjoying passage through the Tracy Arm Fjord, but she didn't believe him for one moment. He was too conscientious to give up solving a case. Relaxing wouldn't be an option for him.

Dora laid out her appliqué pieces without too much effort, but she noticed Briana struggling with hers. Dora was tempted to help her but let the instructor assist. Once Briana understood what she was to do, she began her prattle. Interspersed with yawns, she relived last night's itinerary with Dora, telling her about dancing and dining into the wee hours of the morning. "I simply can't concentrate today. I shouldn't have signed up for sewing. I'm not as experienced as all the others.

Dave insisted I do something to keep busy since he would be preoccupied with his other paleontologist friends."

Dora broke into her narrative. "Dave is your husband? And he's a paleontologist?"

"Yes, he's been one for over ten years."

"By the way what is your last name? Maybe I've read about him."

"Our name is Gleason. I doubt you've read anything. He's not that prominent."

Dora immediately saw an opportunity for questions. "Does he have a special concentration?"

Briana laughed. "Don't think so. He just loves old bones."

"Sounds fascinating. Are you one, too?"

Briana waved away the notion. "Oh, no. I like modern things."

"Is there some sort of paleontology meeting?" Dora asked even though she hadn't discovered one when she had researched meetings earlier.

"No, not a formal meeting," Briana said abruptly and ended the conversation.

Dora would have liked to ask her more, especially about Tron, but Briana busied herself on her quilt. She thought Briana's reaction to her last question odd and intended to mention it to Milton when she saw him at lunch. Feeling deflated on not learning more, she turned her attention to her second appliqué which would be composed of colorful Eskimo costumes, dogs, and sleds. Dora heaved a sigh at the challenging project even difficult for the advanced quilter. She didn't consider the Eskimo's colorful outer wear realistic, but it complemented the pastel squares of the northern lights. She saw Briana sitting idle, staring at the small pieces to assemble and wondered how her sewing neighbor would tackle the task. The sewing instructor noticed, too, as she walked to her side and offered a way out with a simpler pattern.

Dora was tempted to ask for the same pattern but admonished herself for the thought and willed herself to concentrate on her original selection.

At lunch Dora couldn't wait to talk to Milton. The men had selected a spot where they could converse in relative privacy. After a trip through the buffet line, the foursome compared notes. Milton and Anthony acknowledged that they and the authorities had made a considerable dent in background checks and in fact had found several red flags.

"So you weren't sunbathing like you said you would?" Dora asked Milton accusatorially.

"We were asked to help, and we couldn't turn the investigative team down," Anthony defended.

"I know and I did a little investigating myself," Dora told them. "Briana said that her husband Dave Gleason is a paleontologist. I found that to be very interesting."

Milton stroked his chin. "Especially since there are some paleontologists who would like to see that the mammoth tusks that are being harvested should be left undisturbed. In their opinion, the ancient sites are being ruined by the ivory hunters. I wonder if he is of that persuasion."

"Briana insinuated there were several paleontologists aboard. I asked if there was a meeting, and she said no, not an official one and then clammed up. I suppose she realized she had said too much."

Anthony crossed his arms. "I would like to know what Dave Gleason's viewpoint is on the subject of mammoth tusks."

"I will definitely check on both Dave and Briana Gleason," Milton promised.

"Briana told me Dave Gleason was not a prominent scientist so perhaps you wouldn't find a lot."

"We shall see."

Anthony lifted his finger in thought. "There may be another way we can find out more on Mr. Gleason."

Milton looked at him quizzically. "How is that?"

"I noticed a scrimshaw presentation to be held tonight on board. I remember reading Dave Gleason is a speaker."

Milton slapped him on the shoulder. "Excellent idea. We need to learn more about scrimshaw anyway."

The ladies agreed it would be a worthwhile way to spend the evening.

After the group finished lunch they rode the elevator up to the deck to take in the sights of the Tracy Fjord, a rugged landscape of breathtaking beauty carved from glaciers. Hundreds of waterfalls cascaded from granite mountains. From the distance, the Sawyer Glacier invited closer inspection.

For a while Dora forgot the crime before them. The impressive beauty of the fjord erased the uneasy feelings she had been harboring. Milton motioned her to move closer to him as he encircled her in a warm embrace. The warm and strength that he exuded comforted her even more than the scenery.

In about an hour, Dora and Josie reluctantly returned to their sewing class with promises to meet their husbands for a late dinner. Dora noticed almost immediately that Briana seemed muddled about something. She had forgotten the layout that the instructor had organized for her.

Briana looked so pitiful that Dora felt drawn to assist her. "May I help you with something?"

Briana burst into tears at the offer. "I shouldn't have signed up for this quilting workshop. I don't even like to sew, but Dave insisted. He said he would be too busy to spend time with me."

"If you're that miserable, perhaps you could tell the instructor you need to do something very simple."

"She already has. I'd like to quit, but Dave would be upset with me." She wiped her tears and hesitated before she spoke again. Whispering, she said, "Dave has a temper."

Dora disliked being involved in other people's problems, but she remembered Christmas and her commitment and asked, "Is that why you're upset?"

Briana nodded. "We had a fight. I told him I didn't want to sew anymore. He said I had to."

"I'm sorry. Let me help you. My layout is about done and won't take me long to complete. I'll do yours for you if you want."

"I'd like that thanks. Sure I won't set you back?"

"No, it will be fine." Dora set her project aside, hoping she could finish it in the time allotted and helped Briana with hers. When Briana approved of her suggestions, Dora sewed it together into a simple patchwork design. Both had agreed that Dave wouldn't probably even notice that Briana had chosen something less complicated.

While sewing, Dora thought about asking Briana about Dave. Finally, she got up enough nerve and asked. "How long have you been married?"

"Oh, about a year."

"Interesting, Milton and I have been married a year, too."

"Did your husband insist that you participate in this workshop?"

"No, it was my idea."

"Is he here for a particular reason?"

Dora chose her words carefully. She was not about to admit her husband was a detective working on a case that fell into his unsuspecting lap. "No, we are just celebrating our one year anniversary. He knows I love to quilt."

"I see. You're lucky. He seems understanding." Briana's voice trailed off.

"And Dave isn't?"

Briana flinched at the question. "Not…exactly."

———

When the sisters returned to their cabins, they were surprised not to have been met by their husbands. "I was hoping for Anthony's open arms," Josie complained.

"You didn't expect them to wait for us, did you?" Dora snipped.

"Bad sewing day," Josie asked, unaffected by Dora's response.

"I ended up sewing Briana's quilt pieces. She was a wreck today. Guess I felt sorry for her."

Josie laughed. "My sister getting soft on me?"

"Oh stop it." Dora cast an imaginary slap her way.

"Anything happen to cause her bad mood?"

"I take it her husband isn't very attentive."

"I noticed that happening to lots of couples. Probably get tired of one another," Josie reasoned. "Shouldn't be a problem for us, being newly married and all."

"Briana has only been married a year. They should be still on their honeymoon," Dora added.

"Poor lady."

Dora shrugged. "Did seeing the inside passage give you any ideas on your Glacier Bay quilt?"

"Yes. Most of the patterns I have seen are quite complicated. Too involved for a short cruise. But—"

Dora waged her finger. "You're conjuring up something special, aren't you?"

Josie nodded, smiling. "It's not too late to switch to a Bargello quilt. It'll be small but will show my impression of glaciers beautifully."

"I'm jealous. Mine is just a plain appliquéd quilt. Yours is a quilt in motion."

"There is nothing plain about your quilts sister dear."

"I've never done a Bargello quilt before. Just think of cutting all those strips."

Josie laughed "The strips have been pre-cut. Fortunately, one kit had my colors."

"I admire you for taking on something a bit more complicated." Dora said.

"The chart that comes with it will be helpful."

"Will you have time to finish? Our cruise is just about over."

"I was hoping you'd help."

Dora shrugged. "I have my own to do."

"But you're about done with yours," Josie insisted.

"I suppose," Dora conceded. "How long is it going to take you to get ready for dinner?"

"I'm just changing clothes. A half hour at the tops."

"Me, too. Knock on my door when you're ready."

Both women changed quickly into formal pant outfits. Josie appeared in a gold number and Dora dressed in black. Josie frowned at her choice, fluffed her hair, shrugged and led the way to join their husbands outside the entrance of the dining room. Milton stooped to kiss Dora on the cheek. "Have a good sewing session," he asked.

"Not exactly, but I'll explain later."

Their dining companions filtered in and seated themselves at the table. Dora imagined there would be much discussion on the inside passage. Dora thought to herself that it would be an unprofitable night in gathering any more information on their dining companions but listened intently anyway.

Conversation buzzed for a half hour on the sights they had seen today. Milton remained quiet, seemingly preoccupied with his dinner salad. She wondered what Milton was thinking while admiring his fascinating detective mind. To think that once Milton imagined Dora and Josie to be suspects in the art heist case. They had come a long way since then, although Dora had about turned down something permanent with Milton. She was so grateful she had come to her senses.

Dora sighed, giving up on her developing detective instincts when she noticed Milton doodling on a piece of paper. Milton didn't have any significant drawing skills that she knew of. What was he doing? When he had completed a crude drawing of the scenery they had seen today, he held it up for the group to see. "I'm attempting to capture the vision of today in a sketch. Could I get some pointers on what I need to do to pull my masterpiece together?" he laughed at his rendition.

Everyone looked at him in astonishment but no one spoke immediately. An awkward silence ensued. A sense of embarrassment descended on Dora. What was Milton trying to accomplish? How could she help him?" She looked toward Anthony for a cue, but she saw none.

Ted, you must have a knack for sketching," Milton asked him abruptly.

"Me?" Ted stammered. "Why do you say that?"

"I just thought such talent would be beneficial to a curator."

Ted shifted in his chair and reached for his wine glass. "No, no. I hire people if I need an artist."

"Anyone else?"

The remainder of the diners looked at him oddly and shook their heads.

"Guess my own sketch must do," he said as he stuffed the paper in his pocket.

Bridgett spoke up. "You can buy beautiful sketches in the ports."

"You've been to Alaska before?" Milton asked, lifting his brow.

Her husband Bill cleared his throat and cast her an odd glance.

"Well, yes, haven't most of us?" she said defying her husband's strange behavior.

Milton shrugged and looked to the rest of the group for answers. All admitted they had been to the forty-ninth state, except for Dora, Josie, and Anthony.

Over dessert, the diners lapped into silence. Dora signed in relief when the meal was finished, and they walked out onto the deck for fresh air.

"What was all that about?" Dora asked Milton when they were alone.

"I was just fishing."

"I thought so. Fishing for what?" Dora asked impetuously.

"Just curious if anyone could be a scrimshaw artist."

"In our little group?"

"Doesn't hurt to eliminate the suspects. So far the ship authorities have come up with few people to fit the profile," Milton told her.

"Did you remember that Briana's husband is a paleontologist?" Dora said.

"I know there are some aboard, but they appear to have the proper credentials."

"So you did find something on Dave Gleason?" Dora asked.

"No, I did not. I'm wondering if Dave Gleason is an alias."

"I'll try asking Briana some more questions. She was terribly upset about something. I even helped her with her quilt today."

"So that was your bad day?"

Dora nodded. "Seems like it was her husband's idea for her to take the quilting workshop. To me, she is unhappy."

"Interesting. Invite Briana and her husband to dine with us."

"Okay, I will," Dora said as they joined Josie and Anthony by the railing.

"Any comments about the evening, Anthony?" Milton asked.

"It seems they all have something to do with Alaska or ivory. I find that peculiar with such a small group."

"I do, too."

"What about Bill's reaction to Bridgett admitting they had been to Alaska before?" Anthony added.

"I even noticed," Josie admitted.

"Don't know why visiting Alaska before should be such a big deal," Anthony commented.

Milton posed a possibility. "Unless, someone has business interests here?"

"Like ivory?" Dora answered.

Milton huddled into his jacket. "Maybe we'll find something useful at the scrimshaw presentation this evening."

The conference room filled with interested guests. Milton chose seating at the back of the room, so he could see who was in attendance and to study reactions and body language. Dora protested, but Milton shook his head and winked at her.

Ted was introduced as the first speaker. Milton and Anthony were stunned he was associated with this group of paleontologists.

Milton leaned back in his chair. "And to think he was reluctant to give me information about ivory and scrimshaw," he whispered.

"He apparently knows more than he let on when we wanted information," Dora said.

"I wonder why he was so reticent."

Dora glared. "Shush. Let's see what he has to say."

Ted began by giving the history of scrimshaw, telling the crowd that the art form began mid 18th century and ended in the 19th century when whaling was banned. During that time whalers carved elaborate designs on whale bones and teeth with a jackknife or sailing needle. Walrus tusks and other ivory-bearing animals were also used. Carvers applied pigments from lampblack to highlight the details.

"I knew Ted knew more than he was letting on," Milton said, disgruntled.

"Understandable," Anthony reminded him. "He owns a museum."

"Various Native American tribes from Alaska and Siberia are scrimshaw artists," Ted told them. "However, other artists use the fossil ivory for scrimshaw."

That's who we are looking for, Milton thought.

The second speaker, who neither Milton nor Anthony had met, discussed the use of scrimshaw in jewelry and other decorative objects. He showed them examples of scrimshaw artistry. The presenter also mentioned that jade and ivory were used in jewelry and further added that both jade and ivory are exported to China. "China still produces excellent scrimshaw and is a buyer of ivory."

Both Milton and Anthony exchanged glances.

Dave Gleason was the last presenter. He addressed the topic of ivory and the laws safeguarding the harvesting of animals for its use. He began with the complicated regulations to combat illegal wildlife trafficking especially to elephant ivory. "New Jersey, New York, California, and Washington have banned the sale of ivory," he said.

Milton was tempted to jot down notes, but he didn't want to appear conspicuous. He rumpled his forehead in thought.

Dave then expanded on mammoth ivory. Because illegal elephant ivory had been passed off as fossil ivory through customs, several states banned all ivory. Fossil ivory for the most part was legal. Indigenous people could collect the fossil ivory; however other people are restricted to private land with permission. "Collecting fossil ivory on federal land is prohibited, also," he told them.

"Dave Gleason knows a lot about regulations regarding ivory," Anthony said under his breath. "But does that mean he obeys the law."

When the presentations were open to questions, Milton raised his hand directing his questions to Dave Gleason.

"What is your opinion on banning the collecting of fossil ivory?"

"I don't believe we have or will have a shortage of fossil ivory. We have plenty to study, and I see no reason why we can't use it."

"What about passing elephant ivory off as fossil ivory? Doesn't that cause a problem?" Milton pursued.

"Buyers must be diligent in spotting illegal ivory." Dave Gleason turned his attention from Milton and gestured for a question from another attendee.

Several more questions followed, and when the session ended, Milton rose from his seat and took a deep breath. "And we should find out more about the second presenter."

"It seems as if there are plenty of experts," Anthony said. "One of them has to know something about the black suitcase.

———

During the presentations, Otto had been scrutinizing the talent within the room. His scrimshaw artist had requested help with carving the carvings. Since the meeting, Otto knew of several people to ask, but he was hesitant on which one to approach. Whoever he chose, would not be coerced into carving the designs into the scrimshaw. Such a tactic would be too risky; instead, the selected person would have to be tricked into working for him.

Otto paced the floor of his cabin and then stopped to pick up his prepaid cell phone. He punched in a number and waited. "I need to talk to you. Yeah, I know we can't be seen together in public. Otto briefly informed the blonde of what he was contemplating.

"It's too risky," she said. "He can't possibly engrave enough scrimshaw without becoming suspicious of why we are asking for his help."

"It's a chance we will have to take. You know how cranky our clients are."

"You'd better come up with a good story why we need his help. Don't mess this up."

"I'm not incompetent," he roared back and then ended the conversation.

———

The next morning, both Dora and Josie were committed to an entire day of quilting. Dora was hopeful to finish her appliqué in the morning and then help her sister with her quilt.

Briana was another problem. Hopefully, Briana would be in better mood and be able to work on her own project without Dora's help. But then again would Briana accept a dining invitation if she rejected her and not offer any help?

The couples met for breakfast before they parted for the day. Anthony and Milton planned to meet with the investigative team.

"So far I haven't been able to find anything on Briana's husband," Milton confided to Dora while smearing his toast with grape jelly.

"Briana said you might not be able to," Dora explained. "Briana said that he wasn't too prominent."

"He certainly knows his way around regulations concerning ivory," Milton said.

"How about the other paleontologists?"

"So far no one appears suspicious, but that doesn't mean someone doesn't know something."

"Do you suppose we should question them?" Anthony suggested.

"I don't want to scare the culprits away. We have two more ports. So far no one has not returned to the ship. I find that amazing."

"What do you suppose that means?" Josie blotted her lips with the napkin.

"Whatever was in the suitcase is too valuable to leave?" Anthony conjectured. "At least one of our suspects has to be still on board."

"How many are there?" Dora asked.

"We have no idea," Anthony said flatly.

"I don't understand. Ivory is available here. Bargains can be found," Milton reasoned. "My guess is that the person who brought the ivory aboard is working for someone and might get into trouble with his employer, perhaps lose his job or worse."

"In other words, we do have more than one person to look for?" Anthony questioned.

Milton nodded.

Anthony tapped the air with his finger. "Unless, there is more than meets the eye."

Milton smiled at Anthony. "What are you thinking?"

"It's possible we missed something when we examined the ivory. There could be something of greater value that we have overlooked.

"Could be. I suggest we get to our meeting." Milton looked to the ladies. "Meet you at lunch?"

"Count us out," Dora said. "We have a lot to do before our quilts are finished. Josie and I have decided to skip lunch and sew. Meet you for dinner though?" She smiled hopefully.

Milton nodded, and they left the breakfast room parting their separate ways.

As planned, Dora got to work on her appliqué as soon as she entered the sewing room. Sewing machines hummed with anxiety as each participant counted the hours left to complete the quilt.

Briana came in late and appeared to Dora to be as rattled as she was the day before. She seemed that she hadn't had much sleep lately, but she could have been out too late the night before. Dora greeted her arrival but didn't have the time or inclination to question her. Instead, Dora kept her attention on the quilt, hoping Briana would do the same.

Uncharacteristically, Briana said little as she lined up her sewing for the day. She looked Dora's way several times, but Dora didn't invite conversation. After several hours, Dora's conscience bothered her and asked about Briana's evening.

"Boring," Briana replied. "Dave's meeting went longer than expected. I ordered dinner in and went to bed early."

"No dancing?"

"Ah...no. I didn't feel up to it."

"Doesn't appear you are not having a good time."

Briana frowned. "That's an understatement."

"Why would paleontologists book a cruise to be cooped up with meetings that take up the entire day and night?"

Briana shrugged. "Beats me. I came along because I thought it would be fun. Was I wrong."

Seeing an opportunity for questioning, Dora continued. "Does Dave attend a lot of meetings?"

"Yes."

"Where do the meetings usually take place?"

Briana hesitated and eyed her warily. "Oh, here and there. I usually stay home."

Dora continued to push. "Do you have children, a family?"

"No children. I was an only child and my parents are gone. I do have grandparents living."

"Is there anything I can do for you?" Dora immediately regretted her invitation, thinking that Josie should be the one interrogating Briana. She was so much better with people.

"No, thanks. The cruise is about over and soon I'll be back in my New York apartment. I know how to be happy there."

Dora suddenly felt sorry for Briana. She was lonely, Dora decided, and it was then she extended the invitation for her and her husband Dave to dine with them. Briana turned her down explaining that Dave could not be bothered with social engagements.

As promised, Dora and Josie worked through lunch. Dora had put the finishing touches on her quilt and began helping Josie with hers. Briana had taken a lunch break and was still gone. Dora told Josie Briana may have taken a nap. She guessed that finishing the quilt wasn't Briana's high priority.

The sisters made huge progress on the quilt when it was time to call it quits for dinner. Briana hadn't returned, and Dora put Briana's things away, thinking that Briana was unlikely to return. The instructor announced they all could come back in the evening to sew.

The two women met their husbands outside the dining room with special interest in any new discoveries. "Well?" Dora asked Milton.

"Nothing on the paleontologists. Can't find anything incriminating on Briana's Dave." Milton rubbed his eyes. "We must concentrate on someone else."

"Oh, darn," Josie broke in. You only have two days left."

"Don't remind us," Anthony lamented. "Our suspect must make his move soon."

"Provided it's a male," Dora interjected. "By the way, Briana turned down our dining invitation."

Milton frowned. "I expected such a response."

Josie raised her hand. "I have a question."

Anthony nodded. "What is it?"

"How is the suspect going to make a move if he or she doesn't know where the loot is?"

"But the suspect knows we had it," Dora reminded them and then grew pale. "We are the so called 'move,' aren't we?"

Josie shivered. "I never thought of that. Why hasn't he or she approached us?" She looked to Anthony for an answer.

"Possibly not wanting to draw negative attention. There aren't any options left for our perpetrator other than to confront you gals."

The four of them exchanged glances mixed with fear and dread. Here they were once again involved with a mystery that neither of them wanted.

"We will keep an eye on you both at all times," Milton stated quickly. "I apologize for not preparing you for a possible approach."

"Don't blame yourself," Dora consoled. "Try to be optimistic", she added. "Nothing has happened to us yet."

The two couples ceased their private discussion when they joined their fellow diners. Dora felt rather shaky at the prospect of being a possible target for information. She picked up her water glass, hoping to calm her nerves and to her horror she spilled it down the front of her tunic. Milton hurriedly handed her a napkin to wipe away the stain of water.

"Dora, are you alright?" Alicia inquired with concern.

"Yes, yes. I wasn't paying attention to what I was doing," she explained quickly. Milton squeezed her hand in assurance. Dora, grateful for his presence, calmed enough to drink half the glass. The conversation veered off in several directions, but she couldn't concentrate enough to join in. Although, she did notice that Tron was not serving their dinner as he had since the cruise began. Someone asked if Tron was ill. The new server only shook his head.

As usual, Milton was trying several tactics to extract information. Again, he focused on Ted and Alicia because they exhibited the most knowledge on regional art and owned a museum. Milton complimented Ted on his informative presentation. But from their answers to his questions, she deduced Milton was getting nowhere.

Dora ate her meal without relish. She only wanted to leave for the safety of their cabin. When dinner finally concluded, Milton pulled out the chair to assist her. Just then a commotion reverberated through the dining room.

Dora grabbed Milton's arm. "What is it?" she heard herself ask in fright. "Did we hit an iceberg?"

Milton pulled her to him in a protective embrace. He and Anthony shouted options on what to do when someone clearly called out, "man overboard!"

Several diners rushed out to see what was causing the ruckus. A buzz of possibilities filled the room. The members of their dining table hadn't moved yet, undecided on what to do.

Josie clung to Anthony. "What's going on?"

"I'm not sure, but we'll take you ladies back to the cabin, and then we'll see what we can find out." Milton and Anthony pushed past the diners and exited the room. Pandemonium filled the ship, passengers blocked the aisles, and Dora felt panic rising to her throat. She clung to Milton's arm as he broke through the barrier of curious onlookers. Once they reached their cabins, Anthony shouted orders. "Lock the door and don't let anyone in."

Josie wouldn't release Anthony. "I don't want to stay here without you. What if the ship is sinking or on fire?"

"I don't believe that is what is causing the concern. We wouldn't leave you here alone if we thought that was what was happening." He pulled her grip away from him. "We'll be back as soon as we find out something."

Josie shook. "Do you think it has anything to do with us? Or the suitcase?"

Anthony embraced her briefly. "I doubt it. Someone was being careless and fell overboard. That's all."

Dora steeled herself even though she felt the same way as her sister. She glanced at Milton but didn't see the same confidence in his face as Anthony indicated. A cold chill rippled through her body.

Chapter Nine

Milton and Anthony took the stairs to the deck and crowded in as close as they could to the scene of the accident. When the ship's security saw them, they recognized the detectives and permitted their advance. Milton saw that the life saving devices had been deployed, but no one had been pulled from the water. They were told several divers searched under the water but so far had come up with nothing.

"Who saw the man fall overboard?" Milton quickly asked an individual holding a lifeline.

"I believe it's the guy in the green coat standing over there by the ship's security officer.

Milton and Anthony greeted the officer to whom they were already familiar. "Is this the man who saw the person fall overboard?

The officer nodded. "He heard the splash and the call for help," he said.

"But I don't think it was a man's voice," the witness said.

Milton frowned in surprise. "You think it was a woman?"

"I believe so."

"Did you get a good look at her?"

"Not at all. Like I said I heard a splash and a call for help."

"How can that be?" Milton thought out loud.

The officer replied with a shrug, "The current must have washed her away."

"So what happens now?" Anthony asked this time.

"The anchor has been dropped. Can't move until an investigative team arrives and asks questions."

"So we can be here for a while?" Milton asked.

The officer nodded.

"Do you need us to stay?"

"No, I don't believe so. Someone might be missing our victim soon and contact us. For now, there isn't much we can do."

The men turned to leave. Satisfied there was nothing more to see, the spectators dwindled, returning to their previous pursuits. Milton and Anthony discussed what had just occurred. "Do you suppose this was an accident or did someone push her over?" Anthony asked in low tones.

"And does it have something to do with the suitcase of ivory?"

"Whatever it is, while the ship remains stationary we will be given a little more time to solve the mystery."

"Not enough, I'm afraid," Milton said. "We should consider forcing the thief's hand."

Anthony slowed his walk. "How do you mean?"

"By dangling the stolen ivory in front of his or their nose. By now, I'm quite confident there are more people involved."

"But they would know that we're setting them up," Anthony pointed out.

Milton stroked is jaw. "Not if we plan the set up well. Have to think on it."

When Milton and Anthony returned to their cabins, they unlocked the door that was barricaded with a stack of chairs. "It's your husbands." They both called out.

Josie and Dora hurriedly unbarred the doorway. "Sorry," Josie said. "We're scared out of our wits. What did you find out?"

Milton sat down wearily on the bed. "Not a lot. The person who fell overboard is thought to be a woman. No one has been retrieved yet."

"A woman?" Josie asked in alarm. "Was it an accident?"

"We don't know."

Josie rubbed the goose bumps from her arm. "This is creepy."

"Not to worry," Anthony said. "It has nothing to do with you."

"How can you be so sure?"

"At least Milton and I don't think so."

"Then it could have something to do with the ivory."

Annoyed with the pointless banter, Milton spoke. "By tomorrow, we should know the name of the missing passenger."

"It's late," Dora reminded them. Let security take care of it."

With that said the couples separated to their respective cabins. Dora interrogated Milton further when they were alone. She probed for Milton's honest opinion.

"It's very possible there is a connection," he said. "Be vigilant" were his last words to her before they fell into a fitful sleep.

The next morning, the two couples awoke to discover the ship hadn't moved overnight. Divers were still at work in a recovery effort.

Dora and Milton joined Anthony and Josie in their cabin to discuss the recent happenings.

"How long will this take?" Dora asked Milton as she withdrew from the window where she could see the rescue operation in progress.

"I'm not sure, but it will buy us more time to conduct a search for the suitcase's owner."

Josie poured the morning coffee in their cabin. "And I need time to finish my quilt."

Anthony yawned and stirred in a caramel flavored coffee creamer. "Maybe we can find out something more at breakfast."

"I hope they found the woman alive," Josie said sadly. "I wouldn't want a dead body to haunt our vacation."

Dora nodded. "I agree."

"We are going to accompany you ladies to the sewing room this morning," Milton told them.

Dora frowned. "Is that necessary?"

Milton glanced at Anthony. "We'd feel better."

"That's not necessary. No one is going to harm us in broad daylight," Dora said.

Josie tightened the grip on her coffee cup. "Harm us? Are we in danger?"

"We don't know," Anthony said truthfully.

"You two need to find out what's going on," Dora said. "Time is running out."

Josie crossed her heart. "We'll be careful, except I don't know what to be careful of?"

A hard line formed at Milton's mouth. "We're not sure either, but we vow to find out."

Anthony sighed heavily. He was not in his usual jovial mood. An aura of seriousness pervaded the space. "Let's go to breakfast," he said. "We aren't accomplishing anything here."

The foursome chose a breakfast bar for a quick inconspicuous meal. Passengers milled around as if there were no significance events clouding their cruise. "I thought we'd have heard more by now," Dora said to Milton as they buttered their pancakes.

"Not everyone knows what happened last night. Just as well. Speculation rather than hard facts is distracting anyhow."

No one visited much during breakfast; instead, each was seemingly buried in their own thoughts. Milton was disappointed in the investigation's progress. It was as if the perpetrators weren't concerned with their missing loot. Perhaps it wasn't as valuable as he thought. It seemed that they rather lose it than show their hand. Realistically, Milton prepared himself for not finding the answers. But he wasn't ready to give up. He had a plan if nothing else worked.

Milton and Anthony insisted on walking their wives to the sewing rooms in spite of their protests. But once they arrived, Dora and Josie invited the men in to show them the progress on their quilts. "Briana's not here yet," Dora said. "I thought I would introduce her to you and Anthony."

"We can wait awhile," Milton suggested as he studied the quilts.

"If you don't mind. I'd really like you to make your own assessments."

"No problem. I don't have an agenda this morning."

Dora smiled weakly. "I'll tell the instructor you'll be around a while." The men stayed a while longer and then left the women to their sewing, explaining they would be back later.

Dora and Josie settled in, making the most of their time in case the ship would soon continue to the next port of British Columbia. According to the itinerary they would be able to choose from tours of Victoria. But at the moment choosing a tour was far from their minds.

Two hours later, Briana still had not shown up for class. Dora became worried and spoke to Milton when he stopped by. "I have a bad feeling about her."

"It's time we meet her husband Dave."

"I hope you find out something."

"We'll be back later to check on you. In the meantime, Anthony and I will find Mr. Gleason and ask him some questions."

Milton touched her arm and smiled, then left with Anthony at his side.

"Where do we start?" Anthony asked.

'We'll ask the staff for the cabin number, a picture, and whatever information they have on Dave. As far as I know, we are still on the investigative team."

The staff recognized the pair of detectives and willingly issued the information they requested, although no one was reported as missing. "Surely, by now someone should have reported a missing person," Anthony said as he studied the ship's photograph of Dave and Briana. "Do they look like newlyweds to you? I'd say they don't even seem to like one another." He held up the picture. "Sad looking couple, I'd say."

Milton chuckled. "They're certainly not newlyweds like you, Anthony."

Anthony blushed. "Guess not."

Milton thanked the staff for their help and left with Anthony to locate Dave Gleason.

"Let's stop by their cabin first. See if anyone's there."

Anthony proceeded to the cabin number they were given by the staff. They knocked on the door several times but there was no answer.

"What if he's in the conference room with his paleontologist friends?" Anthony asked.

"We'll wait there. He has to come out some time."

"I don't understand what they have to talk about that would take an entire week."

"Me neither. But it must be legit."

As both feared, the conference doors were closed. Both detectives located themselves in view of the doors and waited. "They have to go to lunch. Don't' they," Anthony asked.

"Unless they order lunch in."

Anthony groaned. "How about we get someone to page him?"

"Good idea. That may work. You stay here, and I'll see what I can do."

Within the half hour, Dave Gleason appeared outside the closed doors. He scowled. "What is it?"

Both Milton and Anthony flashed their detective badges. Milton began, "Sorry to bother you, but your wife Briana didn't show up for her sewing class."

"Is that all you want? Are you truancy officers?" he asked sarcastically.

"A woman fell overboard last night. When did you see your wife last?"

"This morning," his tone softened. "She told me she was skipping class today. My wife isn't fond of sewing. I'm the one who urged her to give it a try while on this cruise."

"We stopped by your cabin and there was no answer."

"I wouldn't concern yourself. She enjoys sleeping in, or she may have taken a walk on deck."

"We understand you're a paleontologist?"

"I am."

"Attending a conference on board?"

"An informal gathering of colleagues."

"My wife has been telling me that Briana has been troubled by something, lately?" Milton watched his reaction.

"Oh, that." He stroked his jaw line. "She's been complaining we're not spending enough time together. I warned her I wouldn't be able to while on this cruise, but she insisted on coming with me anyway."

"I see."

"You know how women are? We as husbands never pay enough attention to them."

Milton ignored the question. "Are there any women paleontologists at this informal gathering?"

"No, why do you ask?"

"Just curious."

"I assure you I left Briana in the cabin this morning." He turned back toward the door. "They're waiting for me."

Milton nodded. "Thanks for your time."

After the door closed, Milton asked Anthony for his impression of Dave. "I don't believe he's in love with his wife. I know I wouldn't leave Josie on her own for a week." He chuckled. "She would be furious with me."

"I agree, but it's no crime to be out of love with your wife."

"But it would be if she was pushed overboard."

———

By mid-afternoon, Briana's whereabouts were unknown. The ship's staff had scoured the ship from top to bottom, and she was not found. It was concluded Briana was missing and could be the woman who fell overboard, although no body had been found. Dave Gleason had been notified, but Milton and Anthony weren't there to see his response. The investigative team felt they had done all they could. Without a body the investigation was stymied; however, the authorities halted the cruise ship for a few more days for a recovery effort.

Dora and Josie took advantage of the delay by sewing on their projects. Every once in a while, Dora glanced to Briana's sewing machine, wondering if she was the unlucky woman who fell overboard. She brooded about her disappearance the entire day, admonishing herself for not asking her more personal questions. If she had, she could have prevented her disappearance.

During the afternoon break, she drew Josie aside. The possibility that her sewing neighbor fell overboard affected Dora terribly. "I must be bad luck," Dora told Josie. "I should have helped her."

"But you did. How would you know she was destined to fall overboard?"

"Or was she pushed? No one saw anything. And with no body we can't be sure she is dead. Poor woman." Dora's voice choked. "I should have been more sensitive."

"You did what you could, Dora. It's not your fault."

"I've been thinking all morning, and I have an idea that might put my mind at ease."

"What is it?"

"I know where Briana's sewing locker is, and I'm curious to know if her quilt project is still there."

"Of course it would be if she was pushed overboard."

"But like Milton said, her body hasn't been found."

"You think she could still be aboard ship?"

"Not for certain. But I think it's a possibility."

"But her cubicle is locked. Isn't it?"

"I haven't tried it."

"Someone will notice what we're doing."

"I want you to distract the instructor with a question or something. She keeps another set of keys in the cabinet in the corner. It just so happens she left it unlocked."

"Wow, you're going to risk getting caught."

"I'll think of an excuse in the meantime. Besides, I was helping Briana finish her quilt. It's understandable that I would want to work on her quilt."

"Okay. I'll call her over to me. When?"

"In about ten minutes when we reconvene. First I'll check to see if it's locked."

After the break, Dora waited until everyone was settled with their task. Luckily, Briana's sewing locker was in the same row as hers. She felt confident no one would notice when she left her machine and walked over to her own locker. When the Josie called over the instructor, she left her chair and proceeded to the lockers and stopped at Briana's. To her surprise, when she tried the door it was unlocked. She opened it wider and discovered it had been cleaned out. She was about to shut it when she noticed something green, a small stone amid a sifting of dirt. Dora looked over her shoulder to see if anyone was watching her, but no one paid attention to what she was doing and the instructor was still out of sight. She pocketed the stone and scrutinized the dust. She was certain she had seen this type of dust before.

Upon hearing the instructor's intended return; she closed the door and slipped back to her machine. Her mind was muddled about what she discovered. She wanted to speak to Milton immediately, but she willed herself to pretend to be sewing.

The hours dragged by until the class ended for the day. As soon as she and Josie were outside the room, Josie wanted to know what Dora found.

"I'll tell you when we join the fellows."

Josie brightened. "Look no further, here they are."

Milton and Anthony were waiting for them. Dora smiled in relief and told Milton that they had to talk somewhere secluded. The foursome climbed the stairs to the deck and sat down at a table. Momentarily, Dora sat silent and breathed in deeply of the ocean air.

Dora began by explaining the plan she had formulated at the spur of the moment. Milton couldn't help but smile. "You did that?" he said.

She nodded and reached in her pocket and produced the green gem. "Be careful," she whispered to Milton. "Don't let anyone see it."

He held it in the palm of his hand, rolled it around, and showed it to Anthony.

"Wow," Anthony said. "Are you thinking what I'm thinking?"

Milton nodded. "I think it's jade. What was this doing in a sewing locker?"

Dora shrugged. "There's more to tell. With the jade was dust, fine dirt. Like the dust we saw with the ivory."

Milton looked directly at Dora. "Did you see any jade with the ivory in the black suitcase?"

"No, not at all."

"You probably didn't think to check the suitcase lining?"

She stiffened. "Of course not. How were we to know to look for jade?"

"Sorry, we don't even know if the jade was in the same suitcase. And beside jade isn't illegal, unless it was stolen."

Anthony squinted in thought. "What puzzles me is how they were able to get the suitcase through security?"

"Right. Another big question to answer." Milton let out a low whistle. "Could Briana be our thief? She could be the one who took your stash from your locker and placed it in hers."

"But how did she know we had the stash?" Dora asked.

"Somehow she saw you place it in your locker."

"She did come up to us after we stored it in our cubicles."

Anthony suddenly tapped the table. "So this may explain her disappearance. Somehow she got away with the loot."

"But how?" Josie asked. "And who is she working with? Her husband?"

Dora narrowed her eyes. "So she's probably not dead? And here I was all broken up thinking I should have been kinder."

"Anthony and I have believed that the woman overboard incident was possibly connected to the ivory. Whether she's alive or not is still up for debate. However, theft may prove to be the motivation for her disappearance. But how does the jade fit in with the ivory." Milton scratched his head. "We must keep searching for answers even though the ship will be docking soon."

Anthony shook his head. "Right now, time is our enemy. I would bet with certainty whoever is responsible will flee once the ship docks."

Milton nodded. "And it seems Briana may have already left the ship. But how and with whom?"

Anthony glowed with another explanation. "Or another possibility could be that someone pushed her after retrieving the ivory and the jade."

Chapter Ten

The next day while the ship was still anchored, Anthony rushed into the cabin waving an official looking invitation. "Look what I got." He handed the gold edged card to Josie.

"Wow, an invite to the Captain's dinner. How did we rate?"

"Probably because Milton and I have met the Captain several times. Not that you aren't important, too," he teased.

She frowned. "Very funny." "Oh, I got to see if Dora got one too," she said, rushing out the cabin door into the hall and meeting her sister halfway. Milton was following close behind. "You got one, too?" She squealed with delight.

"I did."

Josie herded them into her cabin. "What are you wearing?"

"The red dress?" Dora glanced at Milton sheepishly. "I have nothing else to wear."

Anthony shook his head. "Why all this fuss? It's just a dinner."

"I tend to agree," Dora said flatly. "I'd rather not go. I don't know what to say to all these important people."

"Just don't discuss any of the strange happenings," Milton advised.

"Believe me, I don't plan to," Dora said.

"We might come up with some clues," Anthony reminded them, reading the invitation again. It's tonight. Kind of short notice don't you think?"

"It is but with all the commotion I suppose it got delayed," Dora commented.

"I'm looking forward to it, too," Milton said. "It's a chance to meet other passengers. Do I need to remind you we have no firm leads on anyone?"

Neither Josie nor Dora responded to Milton's dilemma; instead, they were scheming how to prepare for tonight's dinner invitation with the Captain. Dora whisked Josie aside and shared her need for an accessory for her red dress to conceal her exposed skin. Since there were boutiques aboard ship, they kissed their husbands adieu and left the cabin for shopping.

The women rode the glass elevator up several levels and stepped off to an array of boutiques with attractive glass fronts. Selection appeared limited but Dora persisted.

At first, Dora shopped for an evening jacket, but when she inspected the prices she changed her mind. Josie suggested a scarf. Delighted there was another less expensive option, Dora changed her search. With the help of a clerk, Dora purchased a large red and white scarf which she draped successfully over the blouse she was wearing. "Perfect," she said to Josie. "Although I wished it covered my hips. Are you buying anything?"

"No, my gold dress will do just fine. Shall we have our hair done?"

Dora hooked the shopping bag over her arm and didn't respond until they left the boutique. "Can you imagine what they would charge? Besides, my hair is short what could they do to change its look?"

"Suppose your right. But let's check it out anyway. Maybe they post their prices."

"I doubt it. Most women aboard don't care what they must pay to look glamorous."

"Please, Dora."

Dora rolled her eyes. "Alright. Lead the way."

As Dora had said, the prices for a new do were not listed in plain sight. Josie wilted when Dora suggested she ask about the cost of a hairdo.

"I can't embarrass myself." Josie jerked away from Dora when she attempted to push her forward.

"If you want a new hair style for tonight, you'll have to pay the price."

"I don't think Anthony would approve. Let's get going. I want to wash my hair."

———

The Captain's dining room filled with guests dressed to the hilt. Dora and Josie fit in beautifully with the other lady guests. Milton chuckled to himself when he saw Dora tugging at her large scarf she used as a cape to cover her bare arms and neck. She sat down at the table between him and Anthony. The seating arrangement was obvious to Milton. Dora wouldn't have to converse with a stranger if seated between the two. Even though she was peculiar at times, he loved her. Josie who seated herself next to her husband was already prattling with a guest.

Waiters bustled around serving the attendees red wine before the meal commenced. Two elderly couples were seated across from them, but neither couple initiated a conversation.

However, the guests who sat closest to the Captain were laughing and filled with merriment. Their voices drifted to where the foursome dined on lobster and steak.

"At least the meal is exceptional," Anthony muttered to Josie while dipping his lobster in melted garlic butter.

"I think it's all divine," Josie said, lifting her wine glass to her husband.

He joined her in a toast but practically spilled the libation when he heard a distracting voice. "That voice. I've heard it before," Anthony whispered under his breath.

"What voice?" Josie seemed irritated.

"The woman on the far end of the table. I believe she's the one with the blonde hair. Listen."

Josie wrinkled her brow and strained to hear the familiar voice. "Yes, yes," she said, "I have heard it before." She paused and listened again. "It couldn't be, could it? When we knew her, she had black hair."

"I'm not sure," Anthony said. "Dora, listen to the lady with the blonde hair."

Dora turned her attention to the voice of coyness and laughter. "She's charming the Captain."

"More than that. Don't you recognize her voice?"

Dora listened again. "It doesn't look like her."

"Forget the looks. Listen to the voice."

Milton frowned. "What's this all about?"

"You weren't with her long enough to remember," Anthony explained. "But we do."

"What's she doing here?" Josie demanded. "Perhaps she's looking for you, Tony."

Anthony blushed. "So you ladies agree with me that it's Cornelia?"

Dora and Josie nodded.

Milton caught on. "The one connected with the art heist. We arrested her and her accomplices in San Francisco.

Anthony gasped. "Something must have happened to let her get away."

Josie tried not to stare. "Why haven't we seen her on this ship before now?"

Dora reminded them that they were on a big ship, the size of three or four football fields.

"Or she could have gotten on at another port," Anthony said still dazed from the revelation.

Josie whispered. "Then she didn't bring the suitcase aboard."

Anthony nodded and admonished them to keep still about what they had just seen. "We'll talk later," he warned them.

After the meal, they left the dining room and when away from the guests, Anthony initiated the former conversation. "Cornelia knows how to work the system. And she'll disappear again."

"Surely, Cornelia has noticed us, too," Dora said. "I wonder what name she's using now."

"Better yet," Anthony said. "What is she up to? I'm sure it has to be a crime of some sort."

"It's a big ship," Milton said, repeating Dora's words. "Now that she's seen us, I imagine she will be less visible."

Dora craned her neck to see if she could see her among the crowd. "Cornelia is a slippery one."

Anthony clenched his jaw. "And a suspect. The one who orchestrated my near death experience in Santa Cruz."

"She's the answer to our puzzle," Milton said. "I'd stake my reputation on it. We can't let her get away."

"We have nothing to hold her on," Anthony reminded him.

"We must tail her somehow."

"She knows what we look like. Someone else will have to follow her."

"The ship's authorities can help us with that."

"Or we could disguise ourselves," Anthony suggested with a gleam in his eyes.

"I suggest we return to our rooms and talk." When they had arrived at their cabins, Milton unlocked the door to his and invited them in.

Dora began making a pot of coffee. "Why was Cornelia at the Captain's table?"

"She's an art expert. Remember? "Josie said. "Even if she is a thief."

Dora nodded. "I have a hunch she knows all about Alaskan art, including ivory and scrimshaw."

"I doubt she is working alone," Anthony said. "So far she is the only suspect we have. Odd it would be one of our former ones."

Milton shook his head. "What are the chances of that?"

Anthony socked his fist into his palm, startling Josie. "This time we'll nail her."

Josie nodded. "And her partners in crime."

———

In a few days, the cruise ship would dock in Victoria. Although now that Cornelia was discovered on board, Milton and Anthony had a major break in the case. They couldn't prove anything but were highly suspicious of her presence. Milton had one last scheme to entice her and the accomplices to act and expose themselves, but he needed the help of a security team which remained on ship after the recovery efforts. They arranged to meet in the afternoon.

"Your plan is a risky one," the security leader Jack said after Milton explained what they had planned. "We could lose the last stash very easily."

"I know that sir," Milton said. "But if we don't try, we will never know who is illegally dealing in ivory."

"Good point. Do you have any suspects?"

"I have at least one," Milton further added. "She was involved in an art heist several years ago. We caught her red-handed in San Francisco, but she apparently managed to escape after capture or there was not enough evidence to hold her."

"So you're telling me we are dealing with a crafty thief? Any idea who her accomplices are?"

Milton shook his head. "No."

"In your opinion do you feel the ivory caper and the woman overboard are connected?"

"I can't say for sure."

Jack focused his attention on Milton. "Now, tell me of your plan."

Milton sighed deeply and began. "We noticed at the Captain's dinner that Cornelia, the woman in question, was flirting with the Captain. I believe with the Captain's help we could set up a sting operation."

"Go on."

Cornelia is an alias. She's into art and perhaps could be persuaded to examine the Captain's stash' of ivory."

"Indeed, the ivory that's now in the safe."

"Right."

"But would she recognize it as being the stolen goods?"

"That's a chance we'd have to take," Milton said. "She didn't bring it aboard since she got on the ship in another port."

"So someone else brought it on. But isn't she too smart to bite?"

"She is, but at least she would know where it was and might try to retrieve it."

The security officer's eyes gleamed "I have a better idea."

Milton settled back in the chair. "Let's hear it."

"We have a few GPS tracking devices with us. How about we hide one in with the stash that your Cornelia will examine."

"She might be wise to such tactics."

"She may, but it might be our only chance. The ivory would have to be confined to a box or bag where we implant the device. Then we could track the goods, whether she keeps them or gives them to someone else."

"Sounds too simple," Milton said.

"It might work and it might not, but we had better try it."

"Do it then."

"Let's get Captain Simmons in here and see if he'd help us out." Jack motioned for his team members to find him.

While they waited, they worked out the details of the sting. By the time the Captain appeared, they were ready with the plan which they explained to him. He accepted the challenge with a certain amount of reservation. "What if she puts the move on me? Cornelia is quite beautiful and charming."

Anthony chuckled. "She did that to me once. Just remember she is capable of anything."

The Captain paled. "Now, I'm supposed to feel better?"

"Don't worry. We have you covered," Jack assured him. "Let's put this sting into operation.

—

The Captain sent a message to Cornelia inviting her to a private dinner to help him evaluate his ivory collection. He apologized for the late notice, citing the recent occurrences for his delayed invitation. Before their meeting, his cabin was fitted with bugging devices so the authorities could listen in and record the details. The tracking device was installed in a sturdy box with a false bottom. To everyone's surprise she accepted the invitation and arrived in an alluring black velvet dress slit up the sides to reveal her shapely legs. A large jade necklace ornamented her neck. Her blonde hair fell loose.

"I'm sorry for imposing on you like this, but I realized time was running out," Captain Simmons said, struggling to keep his voice from shaking. He cleared his throat several times. "I meant to talk to you after the Captain's dinner, but I was sidetracked."

"No problem. Will anyone else be coming?"

"Ah…no. I asked, but others were already committed. Besides, I rather not too many people know I collect ivory." She didn't seem uneasy being alone with a man, practically a stranger, although she carried an evening bag large enough to carry an arsenal.

"What can I help you with?"

"I have a few specimens. I was wondering if you could tell me what they're worth and where I could sell them."

"Surely, there are others that could appraise your ivory. I deal mostly with paintings and such."

"Oh, well since you were on this cruise and you're an art buyer I just assumed you would be knowledgeable about Alaskan art, scrimshaw or ivory."

"I'll do my best, but like I said I am no expert. I do purchase scrimshaw occasionally."

The Captain offered her a chair and buzzed for a waiter to bring in a bottle of wine which he poured into glasses after Cornelia was seated. She sipped the Merlot; her eyes followed the Captain's every move.

His hands shook slightly as he lifted a box from the unlocked safe. He brought the specimens over to the table. Opening the lid, he briefly panicked with the ruse in which he was entrusted. Since Anthony had studied a few ivory pieces before he joined the cruise ship, he had instructed the Captain which pieces to display. Captain Simmons brought out the blanks first.

"Would you be able to tell me if these blanks are walrus or mammoth ivory?"

Cornelia stroked each one with her slim finger. "Nice. Where did you get these?"

The Captain felt the heat rising to his face. He had been instructed to say he bought them from a native which was a legal way to obtain ivory.

"I'd like to sell these if you are interested," he said to Cornelia. "Perhaps you could resell to a scrimshaw artist."

Cornelia studied him before she replied. A calculating glint flashed across her eyes. "I don't have any prospective ivory clients right now. I also can't tell you if they are walrus or mammoth for sure."

"Not elephant? I hope."

"No, I couldn't say. Elephant is definitely illegal."

"Oh," he said deflated.

"There are paleontologists aboard. They would be better experts than I."

"I…never thought of them."

"I tell you what." She posed her manicured fingernails into her cheek and batted her lacquered eyelashes. "I know a few paleontologists aboard. If you trust me, I could take a couple of samples and ask them."

Captain Simmons hesitated. His instructors didn't prepare him for this scenario. He debated frantically what he should do. "Why not take the entire box. I believe there is an assorted array of specimens."

"Are you sure? I'll take care of them for you."

He smiled. "Of course, I'm sure as long as you return them."

The waiter brought in a salmon dinner and hesitated about where to serve them. The Captain slid the blanks toward Cornelia. She placed them in her bag until he suggested that they could be stored in the box with the others. He gestured to the waiter to serve the meal. When he left, Captain Simmons removed more of the box's contents.

"I also have these. I was told they are pieces of mammoth tusks. I know they can be purchased in many places. Would they be of value?"

She shrugged. "Some value I suppose. I understand an entire tusk sells for several thousand. You don't have one of them, do you?"

"Oh, no," he said a little too quickly.

"She looked briefly at the specimens and then asked. "Do you have any scrimshaw?"

"I do, but I'd rather not sell it. It was a gift." He reached into the box and brought out two pieces of the ivory artwork.

"I do admire the artist that is able to carve a drawing on ivory." She admired the pieces and then handed them back to the Captain who placed them back in the box.

"I also have a few specimens of mammoth bark. I believe that's mammoth ivory in the raw. Would you like to see them?"

She lifted her chin and tilted her head to the side. "No, I have already seen such fossilized tusks. Rather ugly, I think."

"Those pieces he left out of the box. He closed the lid, latched it and slid the box across the table to her.

Cornelia finished her wine, thanked the Captain for a delightful evening, and promised to return the next morning with an answer to his questions.

Captain Simmons rose from his seat at the table and watched her walk away.

———

As soon as Cornelia left the Captain's quarters, Milton and Anthony came in from another entrance. Earlier, two make-up artists were employed to assist with the transformation of two detectives into ship staff members before Cornelia met with the Captain just in case the tracking device didn't work. Wigs, beards, makeup, and uniforms concealed their true identities although Anthony was skeptical that disguises would work.

Milton rubbed his nose. "Do you have a better idea?"

Anthony shook his head.

Almost immediately the Captain informed them that she was wearing a large, expensive jade necklace.

They stood in front of the computer to see if the tracking device worked. To their delight it was operating as they hoped, but all too soon it stopped at the casino and remained at the spot longer than they had wished.

"What is she doing there?" Milton asked impatiently. "I expected her to take us somewhere, exposing her accomplices."

The Captain shook his head. After discussing the situation among themselves, Milton and Anthony volunteered to perform the surveillance in person.

By now, the security team had joined them and Jack spoke. "I don't believe that's a good idea. She'll recognize you."

"We'll be careful," Anthony said. "Give us a chance."

Not to attract Cornelia's suspicions, they planned to take turns following her. By communicating by phone they thought they would be able to keep tabs on her.

Anthony began the watch. Luckily, the casino was smaller than most. Anthony located her easily and had no problem finding a good vantage point. Immediately, he saw the large jade necklace around her neck, although it didn't surprise him that she could be connected in some sort of criminal activity. He spent several hours watching her play the slot machines from the beverage bar and when she didn't leave, he tried his hand at the slots to blend in. Luckily, the machine was paying enough to keep him occupied.

In the four hours he observed her, she never made contact with anyone, not even using her phone. No one sat beside her, and she talked to no one. And she wasn't doing very well at the slots. He thought it odd she would play the machines rather than participate in high stakes gambling. But then again she could leave the slot machines whenever she wanted. She's playing a game with me, Anthony thought to himself. She's testing us.

The ringing of machines kept him alert. She hadn't moved since she sat down. Why hadn't she left the machine that wasn't paying? He wondered. After several more hours, he grew weary and called Milton to take over surveillance.

Milton arrived disguised as per plan, but didn't approach him. Anthony remained in the casino a while longer playing the slot machine so as to not appear conspicuous. When he was sure Milton was in position, Anthony left.

Milton chose a spot at the bar where Cornelia was in view. He ordered a beer and had barely begun to drink it when she suddenly disappeared. He lost sight of her in an instant. Anthony had warned him that she had the ability to disappear. And now it had happened to him, an experienced detective. He surveyed the entire casino and found no trace and even staked out by the woman's restroom to no avail. Taking the chance of spoiling the stake-out, he called Anthony and told him what had happened.

Anthony was ranting. "I knew it! Cornelia is crafty, but we are tracking her now. She appears to be going toward her cabin. Come to the Captain's quarters pronto, and we'll see where she goes."

By the time Milton arrived, Cornelia had already let herself into one of the cabins. According to the ship's records, only one person by the name of Maddy Green occupied that space.

Milton's shoulders hunched when he sat down. "What's our plan for tomorrow?"

"Hope that she doesn't find the tracking device," Jack said. "If she's unaware of it, she should lead us to rest of the culprits."

———

Otto learned that the security team was looking for an expert to identify the contents of the cache in the ship's safe. He certainly knew what it contained, but debated whether he should offer his services before someone else was selected and case out the safe at the same time. But how to do it without arousing suspicion was the problem. After mulling over the idea, he decided volunteering and showing his knowledge was too risky; however, he knew of someone aboard that could do it without causing suspicion.

In the late afternoon, Otto knocked on the door of a cabin where an artist was busily working on scrimshaw. He tapped lightly, identified himself and waited until the door was opened. A table had been set up, displaying the completed scrimshaw pieces. Otto sorted through the art pieces, marveling at the quality workmanship.

"I heard the ship's authorities are in search of someone to identify the cache stored in the ship's safe. I had thought of going, but it's too risky for me. Would you be interested in making yourself available?"

"And you're thinking it wouldn't be risky for me? I have my livelihood and my reputation to think about."

"I'd pay you."

"No, I won't do it. I haven't advertised what I do. It's best to let it go. If I show up, the investigators are surely going to do a background check on me."

Otto chuckled. "And what will they discover?"

"Not much I guess. I've been above the law until I met you."

"Do you have enough ivory to work with to fulfill the order?"

"No, I'm doing my best to finish up the blanks I have before the ship docks in Seattle," he grumbled.

Otto nodded, thinking of the missing cache from the black suitcase. He still hadn't found it, and he was sure the ladies didn't have it any longer. Not having the missing blanks could be a problem.

"Here, read the letter you gave me and see what it says."

Otto snatched the letter that was given to him with the black suitcase. He read it over again. "The client wants one hundred pieces of scrimshaw delivered in Seattle when the ship docks." He let out a low whistle. "Can you turn out one hundred pieces before then?"

"No. Not even working day and night."

Otto began to count the finished pieces. "How many scrimshaws do you have done?"

"Not nearly enough," he said wearily. "I need someone to help me finish the order."

Otto lifted his palms upward. "Who am I going to get? We're out here in the middle of the ocean."

The artist shrunk into his chair. "I have an idea of someone who you can ask. But this fellow is no crook, so you must approach him without arousing his suspicions."

"Why don't you ask him?"

"I won't incriminate myself. I'm only doing this because of our deal."

"Okay. I'll think of something, but you'd better keep working. My client is unforgiving."

"Then ask soon."

Chapter Eleven

The next morning Anthony and Josie felt the ship's rocking motion. Josie rolled out of bed and dashed to the window, announcing to Anthony that the ship was underway.

Anthony sat up and rested his elbow on the pillow. "So I suppose the investigative team gave up the search. No body has been discovered, and the ship has been permitted to proceed."

Josie yawned. "Bad news for the investigation?"

He nodded. "Definitely. We have more unanswered questions than answered, and we're running out of time."

She reached for her robe. "Yeah, we'll be in British Columbia soon. I hope Cornelia makes a move."

"I guarantee all our suspects will disembark never to return. I suggest we'd better get ready for the day. We have a lot of work to do."

In forty-five minutes, Anthony and Josie knocked on Milton and Dora's cabin. Milton answered immediately and invited them in. Neither of them appeared as if anyone enjoyed a good night's sleep. Dora sat with a wash cloth draped over her eyes, and Josie couldn't quit yawning.

After discussion about the ship's departure, the foursome rehashed the recent developments of the case. Since none of them knew much about jade and its connection to the ivory, other than it was Alaska's official gem, they settled into research.

After a while they pooled their knowledge and brainstormed how it could relate to the case. Milton began the conversation. "What stands out foremost is the fact that China is a buyer of both ivory and jade. Alaska has both, although British Columbia, which isn't far away, supplies the most jade to China."

Anthony's eyes narrowed. "So, in summary our thieves have probably secured the ivory illegally, stolen the jade, and plan to sell it to China?"

"Possibly to someone with a connection."

Josie yawned. "But where's the jade, fellows?"

"I'll bet it was in the suitcase," Milton said. "That's one of the reason they wanted that piece of luggage so badly."

"Then they have it in their possession?" she asked.

"Yes, right now they have everything except for a few pieces of mammoth," Milton said. "But how are they going to get it off the boat?"

"I've been thinking that someone among the staff is involved," Anthony said. "They could move goods onto the ship and off the ship without attracting as much attention as a passenger would."

Milton nodded. "Maybe. We can't explain how the thieves got into our cabins and ransacked them without breaking in unless they had access to a key. Any Ideas who could it be?"

"The Captain?" Josie guessed. "He's a member of the staff."

Milton shook his head. "I don't believe so. Usually, it's someone who is low profile."

"Since Briana is a suspect has anyone noticed her with a staff member?" Anthony asked.

Dora removed the wash cloth from her face. "Tron. Remember we saw her dancing with him."

"Yeah." Josie joined in. "We thought we saw him in Skagway, too."

Milton stroked his cheek. "And I remember thinking Tron seemed familiar with Bridgett and Bill. He waited on Bridgett as if he knew her."

Anthony rose from his chair. "Let's have breakfast first and then talk to the ship's authorities and see if we can find out some information on Tron.

After being directed to the proper personnel, Milton and Anthony settled in to learn what they could about Tron. From his resume's biographical sketch, they discovered Tron was born in China of a Chinese father and American mother. He lived there until he was a teenager and moved to the United States where he acquired work as a butler. He worked in that capacity for several years until he apparently acquired enough funds to attend college. A list of references was included. Anthony perused the list and let out a low whistle. His finger marked the spot. "Milton, look at this."

Milton looked over to the list where he saw the name of Bridgett and Bill McFarland. "Is that our Bridgett and Bill?"

"I bet so. That would explain why Tron seemed so familiar with them."

Milton massaged his forehead. "Do you suppose the McFarlands and Tron are here together intentionally?"

"For sure. Now we know Bill and Bridgett have an agenda, too."

Milton rubbed his hands together in glee. "I'll call my genealogy friend and have her research both. By gosh, I think we're finally getting somewhere."

"She must work fast. Time is wasting."

———

During lunch, Dora and Josie informed the men that they would be spending most of the afternoon in the sewing room, organizing the quilts for the evening quilt show. The men were left to the computer surveillance.

For the entire day no tracking activity showed up on the computer. Milton and Anthony increasingly became disappointed, but Jack pointed out that the box was probably still in her room and hadn't been moved. The hall camera captured Cornelia's image leaving the cabin, but she was always alone.

Anthony sighed. "She's being careful. I have a hunch she saw the ladies and me at the Captain's dinner." He turned toward Milton. "She might even remember you."

Milton nodded. "We must keep a low profile, so Cornelia doesn't see us."

"Our wives aren't going to like not being able to go out."

"No they won't. I'm afraid we've ruined their cruise."

"Circumstances ruined our cruise," Anthony shot back.

Milton drew in a deep breath. "Darn, we forgot about the quilt show tonight."

"We did. The ladies are going to attend no matter what"

"Surely, Cornelia won't be there. She's not the quilting kind of woman," Anthony said.

"Do we dare go?"

"We must, or we'll be in the dog house."

"Oh well, it's too late now to worry about it," Milton yawned. "I'm sure she has already seen us and knows we're suspicious."

"If she suspects we are on to her, she could easily take the contents out of the box. She has to be aware of tracking devices."

"I've thought of that. Our only chance of catching Cornelia is to have the Victoria police tail her as soon as she steps off the ship. We can't do it even if we are disguised."

Anthony rubbed his weary eyes. "So we might as well go to dinner tonight and see what Bill and Bridgett are up to."

"We haven't seen them for a while. Somehow we must drop a couple of questions to initiate a response."

The phone rang and Milton answered a call from his genealogist. "Get this," she began the conversation. "Bridgett and Bill are Briana's grandparents. Briana has used the name of McFarland in the past. "

"What?" Milton asked in disbelief. "I had no idea. This opens up a whole lot of possibilities." He mouthed the words to Anthony. "We never saw them together."

"Her grandparents are loaded. They live in a grand mansion in New York. Bill is retired but made his money in the jewelry business."

"Good work. Anymore on Briana?"

"She hasn't made any waves in the social or financial world. Her parents lived in a little town in upstate New York. Both were teachers at a local high school. They are deceased. From what I can glean, Briana spent a lot of time with her grandparents. She received a degree in geology although I can't see where she used it."

"Fantastic. I believe this case may be coming together."

"I can do more digging if you wish."

"Please do. I need more on her so called husband Dave Gleason and while you're at it, I'll give you the names of others at our dining table. Wouldn't hurt to check out everyone."

When the call ended, Milton relayed the details to Anthony who responded immediately. "Briana met Tron at her grandparents."

Anthony brightened. "Then Briana has a connection with Tron as well."

"I'd imagine they do. We need to find out more about Briana."

"Yes, but what have they hatched up between them? And are the grandparents in on it?"

Milton lifted his brows. "Jewels, gems, ivory? I have a feeling they're a huge part of this."

"But Cornelia and her accomplices have the loot. Don't they?"

Milton raised his brows. "Are they in on this together? Or is one group trying to dupe the other?"

"Right. Briana is a geologist. She might have her own plan."

The men left the computer screen to Jack and returned to their cabin to freshen up for dinner. They arrived back at their cabins to find the woman already dressing for dining. Almost immediately, Dora asked Milton about his day. He told her the break through with new information but admitted defeat with the tracking system.

"I don't know if I can look at Bridgett and Bill without suspicion," Dora said. "I don't dare watch you when you question them."

"And I'm not sure what I'm going to ask yet."

"You will come to the quilt show after dinner?"

Milton kissed her on the cheek. "Of course, I wouldn't miss it."

The couples met in the hallway and proceeded to the dining room where they met their dining companions. The ladies began the conversation about the quilts they had completed, all except for Bridgett who was already harassing the waiter.

Since Bill and Bridgett weren't engaged in a conversation, Milton saw his chance after the waiter left. "I imagine you miss Tron? He seemed to get everything right."

"Tron?" Bridgett said weakly.

"Yes, our first waiter. I wonder what happened to him. Odd, but I did see him in Skagway. Do you suppose he got sick?"

"Well, I wouldn't know," Bridgett said brusquely. Bill hid behind his wine glass and made no comment.

Milton let the matter drop. "I'll ask the waiter when he returns. Perhaps he knows something."

Bridgett fidgeted with her silverware while waiting for the waiter to return with a different salad. He set it down in front of her. She poured on the dressing and poked her fork into it.

Milton lifted his finger to attract the waiter's attention and asked the same question. "Do you know what happened to the former waiter, Tron?"

"I...I don't know, sir. I was just told to take his place."

"Have you seen him lately?"

"I may have."

"Aboard ship?"

The waiter moved away from Milton, nearly tripping on the chair's leg. "I think so."

Bridgett gasped.

———

After dining, Milton and Anthony accompanied the ladies to the quilt show. Quilts, representing Alaska and the far North, transformed the walls into a frozen wonderland.

Josie giggled. "It almost feels chilly in here."

Anthony smiled and latched on to her arm.

Many people were in attendance, including most of their dining companions except for Bridgett and Bill. Milton, Dora, Anthony, and Josie made a cursory pass of the displayed quilts. They noted that Janelle and Tom found her Glacier Star quickly. Its intricate design was easy to find. Dora praised Janelle on her workmanship. Josie was baffled how Janelle could finish it so quickly and asked Dora what she thought.

Dora squinted at the impressive pattern. "I think she had a head start on it."

Milton pointed out Alicia's woolly mammoth quilt on the next row. It was the only quilt with the extinct beast. "It will look great in their museum," Dora said to Josie. "Do you suppose she has been on a mammoth dig?"

"A good question," Milton replied.

"See if you can pick out our quilts," Josie teased the men. "We'll see if you were paying attention when we described them."

Anthony smiled. "You don't think I can do it. Do you?"

"No, I don't. But give it a try."

Anthony rubbed his chin in thought. "I know it has something to do with glaciers."

"Good. Anything more?"

"You switched to a different technique called…called—"

"Bargello."

"That's it. Explain it, would you?"

Josie laughed. "Bargello is a quilting technique that gives the appearance of waves, curves, and movement."

Anthony took her arm. "Okay, let's go find your masterpiece."

Milton squinted. "Now for me?"

Dora stood with hands on hips. "Yes. I'm waiting."

"It's to do with the northern lights, but as I look around I see many quilts with that theme."

"You're right. I'll have to give you hints."

Milton sighed in relief.

"Chose one just for the fun of it."

Milton chewed on his lip, perused the array of quilts and led her over to one with a mass of purple and green. Dora shook her head and then offered a clue. "An Eskimo fishing."

That clue narrowed it down to five quilts. She added the clue of a cabin and moose, and he finally chose hers.

Dora laughed and kidded him about his detective skills. A nearby quilt caught her attention. She walked over to it and called to her sister. "Wait a minute," Dora said. "Josie, come here and look at this quilt."

Josie moved to her side. "Yeah, what of it? It looks like yours except it has an igloo and an Eskimo."

Dora studied the small quilt intently. "It's Briana's finished quilt. It wasn't here when we completed the display."

"How could it be? Briana is gone."

"We thought so, but look. I know my own sewing." She pointed to the portion she had sewn. "Don't you remember I was helping her with it before she disappeared?"

"What's the problem?" Milton asked, overhearing her conversation.

"This quilt. It's Briana's. Someone put it up after we finished the display area."

"Are you certain?"

Dora stood dumbfounded. "Yes, I sewed part of this to help her out."

Anthony became curious. "So the evidence is mounting that Briana didn't fall overboard?"

"Looks that way," Milton responded.

"Why would she be playing that game with us?" Anthony asked.

"Or maybe someone else is calling the shots and Briana is just a pawn."

Josie raised her hand. "I know. The quilt is a signal to us. She needs help."

"Who else but you and the instructor would know this was Briana's quilt," Milton asked.

Dora shook her head. "No one else to my knowledge."

"We need to talk to your teacher," Milton told Dora.

Dora and Josie left the men by the quilt and brought the sewing instructor over to Briana's quilt. She remembered their husbands from the day they spent in the sewing room and exchanged a few pleasantries. After Dora explained about identifying Briana's quilt, Anthony asked her questions.

"Was this quilt here when you left the display area?"

Her face grew pale. "I'm not sure. I do know there were no blank spots when I left. Everything was filled in nicely." She examined the quilt's placement. "Whoever hung this up did it quickly. The quilt isn't even level."

"You haven't seen Briana or anyone that shouldn't have been in here?"

"I'm not sure. Husbands were in here, too, and I couldn't tell you who belonged to whom?"

"Did you lock the room when you left?"

She splayed her hands across her chest. "Most certainly."

"Anyone else have a key?"

"I suppose the staff."

"Can you tell us more?"

"No, I'm sorry. I'm truly baffled."

"If you think of anything, please tell us. We'll be here for a while."

The instructor nodded and left to mingle with the participants.

Josie slipped her arm through Anthony's. "Why do we need to stay?"

"When are you supposed to take your quilt down?"

"This evening at nine-thirty."

"We'll wait to see who shows up to claim the quilt."

"Do you think anyone will show their hand?" Josie asked.

"I doubt it, but you never know."

Shorty before nine, Milton received a call from Jack, informing them that they were currently tracking the package. Milton decided to join the security team while Anthony volunteered to remain at the quilt show.

By nine-thirty, no one had shown up to claim Briana's quilt. "Perhaps someone will come by in the morning," Josie said in an attempt to console Anthony.

"I guess I was hoping for too much. Let's take down your quilts and return to the cabin. I hope to hear something from Milton by then." They busied themselves by removing Josie and Dora's quilt and thanking the instructor for the skills they had learned. Anthony scanned the area one last time before they left. "Briana's quilt. It's gone."

———

Milton returned to the cabin about ten that night. Anthony and the ladies were waiting up for him, bursting with the news concerning Briana's missing quilt.

Anthony lifted his brow when Milton entered. "Well?"

Milton plopped down in a chair, his shoulders slumped. "The tracker followed the package to the bottom deck where the signal stopped mid-way in the hall. The hall camera apparently was disabled as well as the tracker. Neither picked up a clear image or signal of what happened or where it went."

"Did Cornelia have the package at the start?"

"Yes, the signal left her room. But where it is now is a mystery. Did you have any luck?"

Anthony looked sheepishly. "The quilt disappeared right under our noses."

"How can that be?" Milton said perturbed. "Did you recognize anyone in the room with you?"

Anthony shrugged. "We've been discussing who was there at the very end. The only ones we can identify are Alicia and Janelle."

"Could one of them be an accomplice?" Dora asked.

Milton shook his head. "So far we have found nothing to incriminate either of them."

"Did either of them know about Briana's quilt?" Anthony asked.

"No, neither Josie nor I said anything to them."

"So if anyone slipped in and removed the quilt, neither one would be alarmed?"

Dora shook her head.

"Now, we have good reason to believe Briana is not swimming with the fishes," Anthony said in an attempt at levity.

"She has to get off this boat at some point," Milton said. "We must alert all authorities to watch for her."

"As well as Cornelia, Dave and Tron," Anthony added.

Josie yawned. "You don't suppose they'll walk off as if nothing has happened?"

"No one has been charged with anything," Anthony said. "Although Briana would have some explaining to do. My guess is that she will have to disguise her appearance or find a different way off the boat."

"Or they may decide to wait for Seattle," Milton said. "There's no guarantee that they will get off in Victoria."

Dora sighed wearily. "So what's our plan in the morning?"

"We'll be ready when the passengers disembark. Anthony and I will be available for surveillance with the tracking device."

"Unless it's disabled," Anthony added.

"True. If that happens, we'll have to depend on other personnel to do their jobs."

Josie grimaced. "I have a bad feeling that they'll get away."

"If we can get one with the goods we may be able to break the case," Milton said hopefully.

"What do you want us to do?" Dora asked.

"I have permission to station the two of you by the exit. You will watch for familiar faces. When you see someone, you will alert a security officer who will be nearby. He will assign someone to tail that person."

"Even if it's Janelle, Alicia or someone else at our table?"

"Yes. Everyone is a suspect." Milton paused in thought. "Would you recognize the black suitcase?"

Dora looked to Josie. "I don't know. Black suitcases are everywhere."

"Alert the security guards to any black suitcase that might be the one."

Dora thrust her hand over her heart. "You're giving us quite a responsibility here."

"I know. But we have no choice."

"Are you two going to follow suspects around Victoria?" Josie asked.

"If given the chance, we most certainly will."

Dora narrowed her eyes. "And what will we do? People will be coming and going all day. Are we supposed to sit there the entire time?"

Milton grimaced. "Ah, right. I guess we can't expect you to stay all day. One of us will relieve you after a couple of hours?"

"Dora flashed a look of concern. "Well, we can't enjoy ourselves anyway when you might be in danger?"

Milton put his hand over hers. "I don't think we'll be in danger. We haven't found any guns."

Anthony chuckled. "I suggest we attempt sleep and be ready in the morning."

Josie glared. "What are you laughing at? This entire scenario has ruined our vacation."

———

The next morning, the men left early to meet with the security staff. Over coffee and a quick breakfast, Dora confided to Josie that she wanted no part of the responsibility the men had given them.

"I'm not too happy about our assignment, either. If we're lucky, we won't recognize anyone."

"Now what kind of detective's wife are you?"

Josie swirled the last of her coffee in her cup. "Not a brave one."

Before the sisters left the breakfast bar, Milton and Anthony sat down beside them and told them to station themselves by the gangway within the half hour. "Don't worry we won't leave you there all day."

Dora sighed. "Good. I wouldn't mind seeing the Butchart Gardens."

After the men left, the ladies descended the ship to the gangway. The security guard nodded toward them and indicated they were to sit on two near-by deck chairs. Passengers had already lined up for their excursions. Dora nervously looked them over. Seeing no one she recognized, she nudged Josie and whispered, "See anyone?"

Josie shook her head.

For nearly an hour, Dora and Josie watched the line of people stopping to be cleared for shore excursions. Everyone they had met on the ship, except for Bridgett and Bill, Briana, Tron, Cornelia, and Dave were going ashore. "I wonder where our suspects are hiding out." Dora said to Josie.

"If I was a suspect, I would be off this ship pronto, but I really doubt they are going to walk past us."

———

In the four hours that Dora and Josie had watched the queue of passengers leave the ship, they spotted none of the suspects. When Milton and Anthony arrived to relieve them of their duty, they were both agitated. "We didn't see any of them," Dora whispered to their husbands.

"Don't be upset," Milton consoled. "We didn't expect them to be so bold as to depart the ship, but we couldn't take the chance that they would leave without detection."

Josie massaged her forehead. "We didn't see any black suitcases, either. The passengers that left were intent on exploring the city not ending their cruise."

"We appreciate you helping out," Milton said. "Now go on your own excursion, but keep your eyes open."

"We're too late for the tour to the gardens," Josie complained. "Besides, it's cloudy. Not a good day to view flower gardens."

"The fresh air and a nice long walk will do you both good," Milton prodded.

Anthony searched his phone. "I'll help you get you a taxi. The clouds are due to disappear by then."

Dora rose from her deck chair. "Will you remain here all day?"

"I'm afraid so. Anthony and I will take turns if we need to. But I promise to join you before dining this evening."

She smiled and kissed him on the cheek. "Good. I worry about you."

Anthony escorted both women to an awaiting taxi. He waved to them as the taxi drove off toward the Butchart gardens.

Once in the cab, both Dora and Josie exhaled with relief that they no longer were responsible for catching criminals. They said nothing to each other on the ride, but when they arrived and exited the cab and paid the admittance fee, they collapsed on the first bench they saw before they ventured out to explore the beautiful flowers. "I'm sure we won't see our suspects here," Josie said with relief.

"Relaxation at last and such beautiful scenery. I for one am ready for a peaceful afternoon."

"Do you realize we haven't eaten since breakfast?"

"Are you hungry?"

"A cup of coffee and something for my headache is what I need right now."

Dora opened her purse and handed her a pain reliever. She took Josie's hand and pulled her off the bench to a nearby quaint coffee shop surrounded with bright flowers and outdoor tables. They both ordered cappuccinos, soup, and sandwiches and lingered over the meal.

"What do you have planned once we get back home?" Josie asked Dora.

"Only rest and relaxation. This trip has done me in. And you?"

"The same." Josie finished her soup and pushed back the bowl. "I've been thinking of asking Anthony if he would mind moving to Hedge City."

"Really," excitement crept into Dora's voice. "Do you think he would?"

"There is only one way of finding out."

"I would love it if you did come back."

"Me, too. You and I have been together our entire life. It's hard to be separated. I have no lady friends I can talk to."

"Me neither. With you, I know whatever I say will not be repeated."

"Exactly."

Dora sipped her cappuccino. "I have another concern I'd like to mention."

"What is it?"

"Wouldn't it be grand if our husbands retired from detective work? We could actually enjoy a vacation without chasing criminals."

Josie nodded. "And lead a normal life. But I don't want to push Anthony into something he doesn't want."

"I know what you mean. Solving crimes is Milton's life."

"But he has you now."

"He does."

"Perhaps this last caper will tell the tale."

"We shall see." Dora stacked her empty plates out of habit and finished her cappuccino. "I'm tempted to have another, but we'd better get going. Are you ready for a tour of flowers? The clouds are clearing and the sun is shining."

They both chose the three-hour tour, so they would have time to freshen up before dinner. Josie and Dora forgot their troubles for a while as they walked on the sun lit paths to the various themed gardens. They both lingered under the rose garden arches and sniffed the pungent red and pink blooms. "Too bad Anthony had to miss this," Josie lamented.

"I'll take a photo of you and the roses to show him."

The three hours passed quickly, but by then both ladies were worn out from walking. Once back at the ship, they both showered and napped before Milton and Anthony returned.

"Any luck," Dora asked the men.

"A wasted day," Milton said grumpily.

"But there is tomorrow," Anthony reminded him. "And we have worked out a plan that's sure to work."

———

On the final morning of the cruise, Milton paced the floor of his cabin, muttering the plan that the ship's security team and the port authorities had worked out.

Anthony's face appeared drawn and troubled. Josie attempted to reassure him not to worry. "You have plenty of backup," she said.

"They're slippery thieves. I'm sure they have an equally brilliant plan," Anthony said in an attempt to smile. "In an hour, thousands of people will be getting off this boat. How are we going to keep an eye on our suspects?"

Josie massaged his shoulders. "You do have help. It's not entirely your problem," she reminded him again.

Anthony shrugged. "You gals will remain by the exit and watch the departing passengers. Do as you did in Victoria. Keep an eye out for the black suitcase."

Josie narrowed her eyes, thinking that it wouldn't do any good. "Do you really think they'll risk the chance of someone recognizing it?"

"I don't know for sure. Just keep an eye out anyway." He shifted in his chair. "When everyone has cleared out, you depart with the luggage and go to the hotel where we have booked you a stay. Remain there until you hear from us."

"My stomach won't stop churning," Josie confided to Anthony. "I'm just as nervous as you are."

Anthony hugged her before they left their cabin for Milton's. "I know. I hope it's all over soon."

Dora looked up from zipping her suitcase when Milton answered the door. She acknowledged her sister and Anthony. "It's going to be hard to wait."

"Especially when we don't know what's going on," Josie commented.

Milton picked up his sports jacket from the bed. "I don't know how long we'll be gone. We'll get back to you as soon as we can."

"Shall we go?" Anthony asked him.

"Yes, we are as ready as we will ever be."

The ladies went to their point of destination, and the men hurried to meet with the security team for last minute instructions. Before, the team split to their separate assignments, the tracking system alerted them that the box fitted with the device was on the move. Both Anthony and Milton volunteered to follow it. Milton's heart pumped in expectation of where their surveillance could lead. He broke out in a sweat. "This could be it," he said to Anthony.

They left the security of the Captain's office and risked the chance of being recognized. The alert led them to the line of passengers leaving the ship. Milton hoped the ladies would not expose their presence when they approached.

As they neared the area where Dora and Josie were stationed, Milton caught Dora's gaze and slightly shook his head. To his relief she appeared that she understood not to acknowledge their presence.

Milton and Anthony could only see the back of the person they thought was carrying the box in his luggage. They followed him until they had notified backup that they were tailing him.

When they were able to see him clearly, they weren't able to identify him. He was not one of their suspects, but they continued discreetly following him to curbside where taxis and cars were waiting to pick up passengers. Before they could even hail a cab, an SUV pulled up to the curb. A lady and three children got out to greet him, picked up his luggage and deposited it in the back of the vehicle. "He looks like a family man," Anthony said in disbelief.

"He does, but it could be a ploy. But I don't want to waste our time following a decoy." He called one of the team, identified the vehicle and license plate, and asked that they follow the tracking device.

Anthony thrust his hands into his pockets. "Now what do we do?"

For the first time in his career, Anthony lost his confidence in remembering details or even connecting clues together. There was little time remaining to catch the suspected thieves. Currently, there was no evidence against them, but wherever Cornelia happened to be meant something underhanded was going on. That's all he needed to know. He glanced over at Milton for a cue on what to do next, but he was on his phone getting updates.

Anthony paced nervously while waiting for Milton to end the call. From the one-sided conversation, he was losing hope that they would be able to nab Cornelia and whoever was working with her. Suddenly Milton altered his tone, and Anthony's hope returned.

"What you got?" Anthony asked when he got a chance.

"There's some sort of ruckus going on down at the pier. We're supposed to get there pronto."

Milton set the pace, running as if he was in hot pursuit. Milton's long strides outpaced Anthony's thick legs. He tried to keep up, but he gasped for air in sheer determination of not being left behind. He was winded by the time they reached the scene where two men were bashing each other with their fists. Two port security men pulled them apart.

Instantly, Anthony recognized the blonde man who was bleeding from the mouth. "Dave Gleason?" he said to Milton.

"Who's the man he's with? I haven't seen him before."

Anthony stopped. "He looks mighty angry."

"Quick, let's get closer to hear what they're arguing about."

The tall man with the black hair yelled to the officers. "He tried to kill me."

The officer slapped on handcuffs. "I don't think he'd kill you with his fist."

"I don't mean now. He pushed me over a cliff in the tundra. Left me for dead, but I fooled him."

The other officer held Dave back who shouted, "Don't believe him. It's just a misunderstanding. He accidentally fell. Let us go. We'll clear it up on our own."

Milton interrupted. "Not so fast. We need to hold them for questioning," he told an officer.

Dave wiped the blood from his mouth with his sleeve. "Questing for what? We haven't done anything?"

Anthony eyed the luggage beside him. "We'll see about that?"

The officers read them their rights before they led them away. The arguing between them ceased for the moment.

Anthony and Milton reluctantly let the police take the two men into custody but not before Milton had a word with one of the officers. He told him the situation and what they had speculated about Dave. He also informed them that Dave was required to answer questions in regard to his missing wife.

"Just like we thought. Dave is up to something," Anthony reasoned. "The guy who was getting the upper hand has something against him."

"Kill is a strong word. "Too bad we couldn't have heard more. This may be our best lead."

"So they were in the tundra, digging for ivory?" Anthony questioned.

"That would be my guess, too. The black suitcase probably belonged to him. Do you suppose his luggage contains its contents?"

Anthony kicked a pebble in his path. "It will be interesting to find out."

"Cornelia and Dave are probably in this together. Why she would be interested in ivory is a stretch of my imagination."

Milton and Anthony turned back to the ship to look for the unaccounted passengers. So far to their knowledge, Briana and Tron had not left the ship.

"Any word on Cornelia?" Anthony asked his partner after he had taken another phone call.

"She went into a hotel and hasn't come out."

"I hope they don't lose her."

"She's being watched carefully. At least we have Dave for now."

They paced off the short distance to the ship and then boarded. Several police were talking with the Captain on the Lido deck. Anthony and Milton joined them for updates.

The Captain frowned. "We've scoured the ship and can't see any trace of Briana or Tron even though Tron was thought to be on ship. Briana may have drowned as we first thought."

Milton stroked his chin. "I don't believe Briana drowned. How else can you get on or off this ship?"

"I suppose someone could blend in with the personnel bringing in supplies. It's pretty much chaos to get this ship ready for another cruise."

"When are the supplies and food loaded?"

"The ship has to be cleaned first and then loading will begin."

"How long?"

"Tomorrow."

"Do you mind if we hang around the ship through tomorrow?"

"Suit yourself. I'll tell the staff to clean and reserve a room for you."

"Our old room will do if it hasn't been stripped yet."

"Fine. Let me know if I can help you with anything else."

"I don't plan to do much sleeping," Milton said to Anthony. "We'll take turns watching for Briana and Tron. I'm sure they're on this boat somewhere."

———

In the meantime, Dora and Josie watched the line slowly queue off the ship. They had been set farther back from view this time as not to tip off any of the suspects. At times, it was difficult for a clear view of the passengers. Identifying a single black suitcase seemed like an unlikely happening. They had seen several go by, but they weren't certain it was the one that had contained the ivory.

They identified almost all their dining companions and some ladies at the sewing room, but there was no sign of Briana or Tron. Bridgett and Bill didn't make an appearance, either. But to their amazement, blonde Cornelia strutted down the gangway as if she was a normal vacationer. She was not carrying anything appearing to be incriminating nor was she accompanied by anyone in particular.

Dora and Josie didn't dare discuss what they were seeing, but Dora was fearful Cornelia would get away without any idea of what she had been up to.

It wasn't until later that Dave appeared with two suitcases. Neither one was black. He visited affably with the ship's staff and seemed unconcerned that several officers were waiting for him at the shore.

Dora broke the silence. "I'd like to hear what he has to say about his wife's disappearance."

Josie nodded. "Me, too."

After the line had ceased, Dora and Josie gathered up their luggage and proceeded to depart the ship. They then boarded a shuttle for the hotel.

Josie sighed. "I'm afraid we didn't do much good watching the passengers leave." She opened the door to her room and invited her sister in.

"No, they are too clever. I'm sure they disposed of the black suitcase. But where are the ivory and the jade? Do you think it was in Dave's suitcase?"

"I hope someone can figure it out," Josie said. "I for one am glad the cruise is over. Drat our luck."

"What do you want to do now?"

Josie yawned and plopped down in a chair. "Take a shower, watch TV, and nap."

"I agree. It's been an awful day. I have no desire of seeing anyone. I had enough of shady people to last me a lifetime."

After dozing off for a short time, they both agreed that they were hungry and decided to eat in the hotel's dining room. After changing clothes, they left their room and went downstairs where they were seated in a spacious room decorated in browns and blues.

Josie placed a napkin in her lap and sipped her water. "I wish we knew how the guys are doing."

"Me, too. They'll be devastated if they aren't successful in capturing the culprits."

The dining room filled while they ate. A familiar voice drifted across the space, causing Josie to turn and look where it came from. "It can't be, can it?" Josie paled. "What's our chance of encountering her again?"

Dora whispered. "Can you see her?"

"Somewhat. Her back is to us, but I see her blonde hair. And who else has that pitched, annoying voice?"

Dora lowered her head and peered over her right shoulder. "How can we get out of here without her seeing us?"

"Like I said, her back is to us, and I doubt if she noticed us as we came in."

"Do you recognize anyone with her?"

Josie gasped. "Yes, I do. But I don't believe it. I think it's Ted."

"Is Alicia with him?"

"No, I don't see her," Josie whimpered. "What's Ted doing with her?"

"Who else is at the table?"

"No one. Odd, they look serious."

"Oh great what do we do?"

"Somehow get out of here and call Milton or Anthony."

"What about the bill?" Josie asked weakly.

"Flag down the waitress or leave the money on the table. Cornelia or Ted can't see us."

Josie raised her hand. "There's the waitress."

As soon as the waitress approached their table, Dora had already thought up an excuse for leaving prematurely. She explained they had an emergency and needed the bill immediately, so they could leave.

The waitress accommodated their request, and they left the dining room, doing their best not to attract attention. Cornelia and Ted seemed deep into conversation and didn't notice them.

Dora and Josie let out deep sighs as they pushed the button for the elevator. "Quick to our rooms, so we can call Milton."

Dora paced the hotel room impatiently for Milton to pick up. In a barrage of words she told Milton what they had seen. He instructed them to keep an eye on them until he got there. "I'm surprised that they aren't meeting in a more clandestine place."

"For sure. They are there right out in the open for everyone to see."

After Dora ended the call, she told Josie they would have to spy on Cornelia and Ted until Milton arrived.

"Do we have to?"

"Yes, we do. I'm not crazy about spying, either, but Milton said we must."

"Where's Anthony?"

"He's at the dock on surveillance."

Josie closed her eyes and took a deep breath. "But where are we going to situate ourselves, so they can't see us?"

"I don't know for sure. If I remember, there is a waiting room outside the dining area. We'll have to sit there out of view in case they leave."

"If we must. Let's get going."

Dora and Josie took the elevator downstairs. Daring not to peek in the dining room to see if Cornelia was still there, they stationed themselves in arm chairs in the waiting area.

Josie sat on the edge of her chair, holding her hands in her lap. "What if they come out and see us?"

"I doubt if they will speak to us if they do. It's a chance we must take."

In about ten minutes, Milton arrived with two plain clothes police men right behind him. Milton stopped to talk to the ladies. They told him Cornelia was still in the dining room. After a brief consultation, the undercover policemen approached the dining room to be seated near Cornelia's table.

"Thanks for remaining here,' Milton said to the ladies, but it's best we return you to the hotel and leave the police to see what they can find out." He took Dora by her hand and walked to the elevator. Once on the third floor, Josie followed Milton and Dora to their room.

Dora brewed a pot of hotel coffee, before Anthony called Milton for his assistance.

The ladies listened to his conversation and by the tone of his voice; Josie knew he was elated about something.

"I must go," he told the ladies. "Anthony's on to something. I hope it's a break in the case."

Chapter Twelve

Anthony pulled a candy bar from his pocket, unwrapped it, and bit off a piece. Caramel ran down his fingers.

He unabashedly licked the caramel from his hand and considered finding a lavatory where he could wash his sticky fingers. He looked up and down the dock to see if anyone was in view. It looked clear. He dashed to the nearest restroom and quickly soaped up his hands, rinsed, and partially dried them. Afterward, he rushed to his post just in time to see Bridgett and Bill. Stepping out of sight, he watched and debated about following them.

Anthony had only a few minutes to decide whether to follow Bridgett and Bill. Soon they would be out of sight. Even though he wasn't sure if he was doing the right thing, he left his assigned post and followed discreetly behind them. They seemed to know where they were going for they were in a hurry. They led Anthony through what he thought was the service corridor. Personnel dressed in staff uniforms scurried back and forth in the passageway. He thought it odd that Bridgett and Bill would be in the service passage where passengers wouldn't ordinarily be allowed. Soon he saw them knocking on the door of a room. It appeared to Anthony that someone who looked like Tron answered the door. The door quickly closed and Anthony stood motionless not knowing what to do next.

A staff member passing him in the hall stopped to ask what he was doing in the corridor. Anthony stammered for the right words. "I guess I'm lost. I followed an acquaintance to this room. Whose cabin is this?" He pointed to the door in which Bill and Bridgett entered.

"It's a staff cabin. But there is no one there."

Anthony persisted. "Someone answered the door."

The staff member stared at him. "You must be mistaken. Besides, passengers are not permitted here. You must leave."

Anthony had to find out who was in the cabin. He waited until the staff person left and then frantically looked around for a place he could conceal himself and yet keep an eye on the cabin. A cart with a flowing white skirt stood nearby unoccupied. He crouched down behind it and called Milton. Once Milton picked up, Anthony explained his situation and asked for advice.

"I suggest we wait outside the corridor and remain until Bridgett and Bill leave. We can attempt to question them, although they might refuse. Do we have anything to hold them on?"

"Not that I know of. I can't stay where I am. Someone will need this cart, and I'm going to look mighty silly as well as suspicious."

"Tell me where to meet you."

Anthony explained where the service corridor entrance was located. After Milton ended the call, Anthony appeared from behind the cart, hurried down the hall, and waited outside the corridor until Milton arrived.

"I had no idea that this lead to the service center."

"Me either, but Bill and Bridgett knew."

"Do you think they're meeting with Briana and Tron?"

Anthony nodded. "I'd bet my life on it. Well not my life, but I'm quite sure of it. The man who answered the cabin door looked a lot like Tron."

"Okay, then, let's find a place out of sight where we can see people coming and going," Milton said. "I hope this is where they'll come out."

"Anything else new on the case?"

"Yes, in fact there is. I'll tell you when I get there."

Anthony remained hidden behind the cart for a few more minutes and when the hallway became empty he left his hiding place to meet Milton. As soon as Milton arrived, twenty minutes later, Anthony questioned him about the recent developments.

"While our wives were dining in the hotel, they spotted Cornelia and Ted having lunch together and deep in conversation."

"Ted doesn't seem the type for an affair."

"No, not an affair. A business deal perhaps. Two plain-clothes police were in the process of getting seated close to them to see if they could pick up on their conversation. I'm anxious to see if they find out anything."

"Ted doesn't seem the criminal type, either," Anthony said. "Anyway, I didn't have him pegged as such."

"Me neither. There has to be another explanation."

Anthony sighed. "We'd better have a plan when we see Bill and Bridgett."

"I say we show them our badges and attempt to question them and see if they'll tell us something."

The men waited an hour before they saw Bill and Bridgett coming through the service corridor entrance, wheeling two blue suitcases. Milton and Anthony stepped in front of them and flashed their badge, startling them. Bridgett turned white and Bill stuttered an explanation. Bridgett told him to shut up.

"We just want to ask you a few questions," Milton began.

"You're the police?" Bridgett asked.

"Detectives."

"We haven't done anything wrong," Bill sputtered while Bridgett glared at him.

"We aren't accusing you of anything. We're concerned about the disappearance of Briana and Tron."

"We haven't seen them," Bridgett snipped."

"We know that Briana is your granddaughter. You must be worried about her."

Anthony noticed Bridgett's shoulders slump. His intuition told him she was ready to talk. "Let's find a place where we can sit." He led them over to a patio table and chairs.

"We have nothing to say," Bridgett said weakly.

"I believe we can help you," Milton said in his most reassuring voice.

Bridgett's eyes darted to her husband who didn't seem to acknowledge her one way or the other.

Milton settled back in his chair. "Now, let's suppose Tron and Briana are in a cabin in the service corridor." He nodded toward Anthony. "Anthony saw Tron open the door."

Bridgett gasped.

"Now as you know no one has seen either Tron or Briana since Briana supposedly fell overboard." He waited for a response. Neither Bill nor Bridgett said anything.

"Obviously the two are hiding," Anthony said, continuing the inquiry. At this point he was unsure of what to say next. He didn't know from whom they were hiding. Neither Bill nor Bridgett was going to confirm his suspicions. Furthermore, he would have liked to see inside their suitcases which they nervously guarded.

———

As soon as Bridgett and Bill realized Milton had nothing more to say to them, the couple stood, took their baggage in hand, and left the ship without a backward look. They didn't speak to each other until they checked into a hotel room. Since they were under suspicion, they had been instructed not to leave Seattle; otherwise they would have left for New York immediately.

When they were settled in and the door to their room securely locked, they looked at each other in terror. "What are we going to do?" Bridgett said to her husband. "They know we are involved somehow."

"So far, we have done nothing wrong except to withhold evidence, aid and abet and…" Bill sat down and held his head. "You're right. We're in deep."

"So what do we say to the authorities? They're bound to keep at us until we tell them what they want to hear."

"Nothing until we know Briana's safe and out of harm's way."

"The detective said he saw Tron in the doorway."

"What if he thinks he did? We didn't confirm it," Bill growled. "Tron and Briana surely know they must leave the cabin or find somewhere else to hide. Don't worry. Briana will let us know where she is."

Bridgett stood close and glared at her husband. "Why didn't you say no to Dave Gleason in the first place?"

"You know I couldn't say no and endanger Briana or us. Gleason isn't one to be double crossed."

"But our ruse of Briana falling overboard worked. Dave wasn't able to find her. He's in custody, so he can't hurt us, anymore."

"But you forget there are others in cahoots with him," Bill reminded her. "I'm not sure who they are. I have their scrimshaw order, and I don't know if Dave's accomplices know who I am."

Bridgett froze at his surprise. "You mean it's here with us? Along with the ivory Briana brought us for safe keeping?"

Bill nodded. "I was supposed to meet Dave after we got off the ship to give him the scrimshaw. But that didn't happen."

"This entire situation is worse than I thought," Bridgett wailed. "We're doomed."

"Not unless Tron and Briana find us first."

Bridgett's tone was coarse. "Tron and Briana will never get to us before the authorities discover we have two suitcases filled with ivory."

"Unless, one of Dave's accomplices steals it from us."

"They would be doing us a favor."

Chapter Thirteen

Cornelia leafed through a pile of papers, pulled one out, and flashed a smile across the table at Ted. She watched him as he perused the sheet. The tusk he wanted was expensive, and she wondered why he would make such a purchase. He didn't look like a high stakes client to her. She recalled that during the time they spent together at the paleontologist meetings, Ted had discovered that she was a connection to what he wanted. He was small potatoes compared to what she usually dealt with, but she thought she'd humor him. The big deal makers were to meet with her shortly, and she wanted him out of the way when they arrived.

Ted shook his head. "I'm interested in a large mammoth tusk for my museum, but I wasn't prepared to spend several thousand dollars to acquire this prehistoric relic, although," he paused. "It would look great to have it on display in my Maine museum."

"Believe it or not, they are going fast," she said. "You'll need to make up your mind right now." She raked her nails through her glossy, blonde hair.

"I just don't know."

She furrowed her brows. "How about if I throw in some extra scrimshaw blanks in addition to the ones you have already bought."

Ted pursued his lips. "How many?"

Cornelia shrugged. "Do you have any use for jade?"

"Jade? You have jade, too?"

"I do, but I would appreciate your keeping our transactions secret. I only have a limited supply."

"How long before it's delivered?"

"Actually, I have the scrimshaw blanks and the jade with me. The tusk will be shipped."

Cornelia wrote out an amount and shoved it across the table to Ted, whom she regarded as being boyishly pesky.

"I really don't want the jade, but I am most interested in the ivory blanks."

"Alright then." She scratched out the dollar amount and wrote another and held it up for him to see.

He hesitated while Cornelia tapped her foot. "I can do that. I'll pay when it's delivered."

"Half now and half later," she said flatly.

Ted nodded and handed her his credit card. "When and where do I pick up the merchandise?"

"It will be delivered to your hotel. I assume you have checked in somewhere?" She handed him his card and stood to shake his hand.

Just as he turned to leave, two Oriental men came to the table, the potential buyers Cornelia was waiting for. China was a large purchaser of ivory as well as jade. Cornelia had connections to both. She anticipated that the men intended to make large purchases, and she was ready.

———

The next day, Anthony and Milton met with the officers who interviewed Dave and Joe. Milton confided to the authorities that they believed Tron and Briana were on the ship. Immediately, the interrogation team sent someone from the precinct with a warrant to search the staff cabins for Tron and Briana.

"Did you come up with anything?" Milton asked one of the interrogating team named Jim.

"Have a seat. Coffee?"

Both Milton and Anthony nodded.

Jim became the spokesman for the interrogating team. "We have more than one interrogator," he told them. "The hours get long. He's in the room with Dave now."

Jim, a seasoned veteran with a mass of unruly gray hair, poured the coffee and then told Milton and Anthony that after five hours of interrogation they still weren't able to charge both Dave and Joe with illegal ivory acquisition on federal lands although Dave Gleason didn't use his real name when he was on the tundra. He was otherwise known as Otto.

Jim sat in his chair and opened two sugar packets and poured them into his cup. He continued with the interrogation results. "Dave didn't admit to procuring fossil ivory illegally although Joe said they had. Dave refused to acknowledge that he attempted to kill Joe, his accomplice. His version differed from Joe's. Dave stuck to the story that Joe slipped and fell over the mountain's edge. Thinking the fall killed him, Dave said he called to him but received no answer so assumed Joe was dead and it was too dangerous to go after the body. Joe, however, was adamant that Dave pushed him over the edge."

"Who do you believe?" Milton asked, thinking the two sugars added to Jim's jitters.

"I lean toward Joe. He was definitely angry."

"I agree with you; however I had no idea Gleason was capable of attempted murder."

"According to Joe, after he miraculously came to without any broken bones, he climbed back up the mountain and walked to the base camp with a sprained ankle, but when he arrived no one was there. He said he stayed there for several days until he could travel."

Anthony shifted in his chair. "So there has to be more to this than a suitcase full of specimens?"

"Exactly. I have my men casing the warehouses and other places of storage. With this many suspects on our list, there has to be something big coming down."

Jim rose from his chair. "Another matter is the disappearance of Briana. Would you two like to listen in on this one? Even after intensive interrogation, Dave still has not shed any light on his wife's disappearance."

Both Milton and Anthony nodded. Jim led them next to the interview room where they had visual and auditory access.

Through the two-way mirror they could see Dave sitting at a table; the interviewer sat across from him. "She fell overboard," Dave said, holding his head in his hands. His appearance was less confident than what Milton and Anthony remembered. Sheer determination prevented him from breaking.

The interrogator didn't back off. "And what about Tron? He disappeared, also?"

Dave glared in defiance. "Who is Tron and what's he got to do with my wife?"

"We happen to know that Briana is the granddaughter of Bill and Bridgett McFarland. Tron worked for them."

"Oh that," Dave said annoyed.

"You and your wife have only been married a year."

"That's right. What of it?"

"From Joe's description the woman at the camp waiting for you does not match Briana's description. Who is she?"

Dave spat his words. "When is it illegal to have a woman companion?"

"It isn't. Odd for newlyweds though. Your wife's grandparents are quite wealthy. They wouldn't have any problem funding a project for their granddaughter's husband. Would they?"

"Just because they're rich doesn't make me guilty?"

"We want to know how this other woman fits in with the illegal ivory."

"How can you accuse me of taking illegal ivory? Have you found it? Where's the proof?" He extended his empty hands.

"Joe told us that is what you were doing."

"It's his word against mine. I'm a paleontologist. He's just a bum with no real job."

The questioning continued for another fifteen minutes, but with no real results, the interview ceased for the meantime.

Anthony narrowed his eyes. "So Dave really is a paleontologist?"

"He is," Jim said. "An unscrupulous one. But knowing the trade, gives him the advantage of taking part in illegal activities."

"The conference onboard was legit?" Milton asked.

"It was. But again, Dave could have been gleaning important information and perhaps taking orders under the table. With a little more research, I believe we can connect him to other illegal activities. Perhaps even elephant ivory trade. You may be aware that elephant ivory has been passed off as fossil ivory. I believe we all have perhaps cracked a case that has been ongoing for some time."

"Good luck with that," Milton said. "He doesn't appear he's ready to talk."

Jim shook his head. "We have a few more people to question, like Ted."

Milton sat up straight. "Cornelia? Do you have any leads on her?"

"We know she has criminal record. We're tracking her and will bring her in for questioning soon. We were hoping she'd lead us to more suspects."

"And then there's Tron and Briana if we can find them," Milton added.

"Bridgett and Bill could give us more insight, too," Anthony said. "But we must be quick before anybody leaves the area."

Jim nodded. "No need to worry. I have them all under surveillance except for Tron and Briana, of course." Jim's phone rang, and he answered, giving thumbs up to the fellows. "They found Tron and Briana and are bringing them in for questioning."

Milton and Anthony both gave each other a high-five. "Where did they find them?"

"In among the trash that was taken off the ship. They were apparently looking for a way off the ship without being seen."

Milton chuckled. "Was any illegal ivory found? It had to be somewhere on the ship."

"They didn't say, but I'm anxious to see Briana's take on all this."

———

Since no more questioning would occur that day, Milton and Anthony left the precinct to join their wives at the hotel. The suspects were under surveillance, so the men decided it might be wise to check in with the ladies. Milton called ahead to tell them they would be there within forty-five minutes and to be ready for the evening meal. He thought he heard squeals of delight on the other end of the phone.

After answering the ladies questions and telling them Briana and Tron were in custody, Milton and Anthony showered and dressed for an evening meal downstairs in the dining area. Once they ordered, the men told them what was transpiring.

"I can't believe you found Briana," Josie said relieved.

Dora nodded. "I was afraid she might have drowned."

"She'll be questioned tomorrow," Anthony said.

Josie kissed Anthony on the cheek and smiled. "Looks to be a busy day and maybe all this will be over soon."

Anthony patted her hand. "I'm ready to solve this case and be on our way home."

"Me, too." Josie sighed. "It hasn't been the vacation we planned."

Milton squeezed Dora's hand. "Thanks to you gals for spotting Cornelia and Ted. That was indeed a lucky break."

Dora blushed. "Have you talked to them yet?"

"No, not yet. That will be on tomorrow's agenda. I don't believe she will lead us to anyone else. But we might as well see what lies she has for us."

Anthony sipped his cocktail while deep in thought. "We believe she is involved with Dave, but there is no way they are going to get together now and make a plan to elude us. We need evidence."

Milton smiled confidently. "An advantage for us. Neither will know what the other said."

Dora closed the menu. "Who else would have some answers?"

Milton answered her question. "We must find out what Ted and Cornelia were talking about in the dining room. The undercover police haven't told us what transpired between Ted and Cornelia at the table. And there are the two Oriental men who came in later and sat at the table with Cornelia. There is also Bridgett and Bill who haven't contributed any information, but they knew where to find their granddaughter and their former servant, Tron."

Anthony frowned. "And there's one detail we can't answer. Where is the ivory?"

―――

The next day another round of interrogation began. Briana looked haggard when she was led into the room. Tremors overtook her body, and she tugged at her arms and legs in an attempt to control her trembling. The first thing she wanted to know was the whereabouts of her husband Dave.

"He's not going to interfere with us," Jim reassured her. He noticed she calmed down some and apparently was apprehensive about Dave. Jim began the questioning.

"There's a lot you need to tell us. First, were you on the deck on the evening of your disappearance and were you alone?"

"I...I needed fresh air, so I went out on the deck and stood by the rail. I was facing the water when I felt someone pick me up and hurl me overboard."

"Did you get a glimpse of who it was?"

"No, I just remember someone was wearing dark clothing and was very strong."

"You didn't fall overboard?"

She hung her head. "No, I was pushed."

"Any idea who did it?'

"I'm not sure, but I think it was my husband." She twisted her wedding ring.

"Dave Gleason?"

"Yes."

"Why would he want to hurt you?"

"I don't know."

"You must have some idea. An argument perhaps?"

"No, not that I remember. He ignores me."

"How did you prevent yourself from drowning?"

"I...I swam back to the ship."

"You must be a strong swimmer."

"I am. I guess."

"What did you do then?" Jim cleared his throat. "Once you got back to the ship."

"I don't really know. Everything was a blur."

"Did someone help you? Throw a life-line or something?"

"I think so. I don't remember."

"What did you do once you got aboard the ship? Did you return to your cabin?"

"I don't think so."

"How did you end up in Tron's cabin?"

"He must have helped me."

"You did know Tron before this cruise?"

She remained silent.

"We are aware that Bridgett and Bill are your grandparents. You know Tron from his employment with them."

"Oh."

"Yes. We know about illegally procured fossil ivory. It's to your advantage to tell us what you know. The answers will come out." Jim rose from his chair and paced the floor. "Now, let's start again." He bent and looked her square in the face. "You're afraid of something. What is it?"

Briana cried out, "My husband."

"Why."

"He pushed me over the edge of the ship."

"Are you certain it was your husband? Did you see him?"

"No."

"For what reason would he push you over the edge?"

She wiped her eyes and attempted to control the sobs choking her throat.

"I know too much."

"About what?"

"The ivory."

"The illegal ivory?"

She nodded.

"What exactly do you know about it?"

"I know he married me for my money to fund his illegal activities. He's not a nice man and never has been in love with me." She sobbed uncontrollably. Jim was flustered on what to do. He waited.

Finally, she spoke between sobs. "I found out about his trip to the tundra to hunt for ivory on federal lands. He had a woman and another man with him."

Jim softened his approach. "How did you find out?"

"He left his email open on his Ipad. I read it."

"Did you know he was involved in other illegal activities before this one?"

"Not for sure, but I did know he married me for other reasons than love."

"How does Tron figure into all this?"

Briana hesitated. "I did know Tron from my grandparents. He's the one who pulled me up from the water. I told him what happened, and we figured it would be best to keep it a secret and pretend I had drowned."

"Did you tell your grandparents?"

"In a few days, I sneaked to my grandparent's quarters and told them what happened. I didn't want them to worry."

"What were your plans when the ship docked?"

"We were just going to wait in hopes Dave would leave and forget about me, assuming I was dead. Do you have him in custody?"

"We do. You'll be safe."

Her weeping ceased. "What about the women and man with him?"

Jim didn't understand what other women were involved. "Did you know them?"

She shook her head.

"Do you know where the ivory is right now?"

"Some of it."

"What do you mean?"

"I took some of it out of a sewing locker. Two women had hidden it."

Now he knew what other women she implied. It was Dora and Josie.

He stared at her as if attempting to peer into her soul. "What were you going to do with the ivory?"

She shrunk under his gaze. "Give it to the proper authorities."

"Where is it now?"

"Hidden in Tron's cabin."

"The cabin was searched and no ivory found."

"I don't know anything about that."

After Jim ended questioning Briana, he motioned to another officer to remove Briana. He sat at his desk for a while going over Briana's answers and then penciled in a time to question Tron. He drummed his fingers on his desk. Would Tron tell the same story?

———

The next morning Jim prepared to question Tron. He perused his notes before he joined Tron in the interrogation room. A search had been made of Tron's cabin and no ivory had been found. This mere fact presented a challenge in questioning Tron. When Jim walked in the sterile room, Tron appeared as haggard as Briana.

Jim approached him with a smile and sat down across the table from him. "Tron would you please tell me what happened on the night that Briana fell overboard."

Tron straightened from his slumped position. "She didn't fall. She was pushed."

Jim lifted his brows. "Did you see her being pushed?"

"No."

"So she could have fallen on her own?"

"I suppose, but Briana insists she was pushed, and I believe her."

"Who do you believe pushed her?"

"Briana thinks it was her husband."

"Do you believe he would do such a thing?"

"I don't know him very well, but I know Briana has been unhappy and frightened."

Jim rose and scooted his chair under the table and paced. "I know you worked for her grandparents for a time. How well do you know Briana?"

"I waited on her when she came to visit her grandparents. She brought her husband, then fiancé, to meet her grandparents. They thought a lot of each other. I had the distinct feelings her grandparents didn't care for Dave Gleason. I didn't care for him, either. He was rude. We all knew Dave did not love her."

"Briana says you pulled her from the water. What were you doing on deck?"

"I...heard about a woman falling overboard. I was outside and offered my assistance."

"Did anyone see you pull her to safety?"

Tron shook his head.

"Why did you keep her rescue a secret?"

"Briana wanted it that way. She was sure it was her husband, and we thought she should be hidden away. Her husband would think she had drowned."

"So why did you quit working in the dining room?"

"Dave knows I'm acquainted with Briana and her grandparents. He would be after me for information. It was best for me to hide out, too. The ship's service team helped us by not reporting where I was."

"Did you team members know you rescued Briana?"

Tron averted his eyes. "No."

"Briana told me some ivory was hidden in your cabin." Jim wheeled abruptly and thrust his face into Tron's. "It's not there. Where is it?"

Tron gulped in air. "I don't know anything about any ivory."

"You must. Briana said you hid it in your cabin."

"Oh, you mean the stash she found in a sewing locker. I doubt it was worth much."

"I'm happy you remember. Where did you hide it?"

Tron shrugged. "Under my bed."

Jim clenched his jaw. Tron wasn't about to cooperate. "I find it interesting that you are on the same cruise as your former employees. Was this arranged?"

"No, I just happened to be working on this ship."

"I don't believe you. There are far too many coincidences here."

———

After Jim ordered in lunch, he marked off a name on his list. "It's time we talk to Ted," Jim suggested to Milton and Anthony. "What do you know about him?"

"We only know that he had been our dining companion on this cruise. He and his wife Alicia have traveled quite a bit. They are interested and collect regional artwork and are curators of a museum," Milton told Jim.

"They seem like ordinary folk. Dress simply and aren't a bit ostentatious," Anthony added. "Hard to believe he and his wife would be crooks."

Ted's face was awash with emotion when he was brought into the police station. He had been told that he was not to leave the city as he was considered a person of interest.

As soon as he saw Milton and Anthony he brightened some. "I don't understand why I have been detained. And what are you two doing here? Are you being questioned, too?"

Milton smiled apologetically. "Anthony and I are detectives."

Ted sat down weakly in the proffered chair. "I still don't understand. What have I done wrong?"

Jim took over. "You were seen talking to one of our suspects. We just want to know what the topic of interest was."

"And who would that be?"

"We know her as Cornelia although she uses other names. She's the blonde lady you met at the hotel restaurant."

"Oh. The nice looking lady who knows a lot about museums and artifacts? Her name is Maddy."

"She's the one. Where and when did you first meet?"

"The night of the conference when I spoke on scrimshaw."

"Did she approach you?"

"Yes, she told me she had ivory pieces that I might be interested in."

"What were you two discussing at the hotel?"

Sweat beads formed on Ted's face. "I just wanted to buy a mammoth tusk for my museum. Before we finished the transaction, I had also bought scrimshaw blanks. She offered to sell me jade, but I have no use for jade. It wasn't illegal was it?"

"We believe the fossil pieces and the jade were secured illegally. Did you give her the money?"

"Half of it. The other half when I received the shipment. But I didn't know it was illegal," Ted protested. "You must believe me. Will I be prosecuted?"

"We'll leave that to the court. You will have to testify at some point."

Ted shook his head in defeat.

Milton redirected the conversation to the ivory blanks. "What do you do with ivory blanks?"

"I'm a scrimshaw artist."

"Why didn't you say something about your ability when we casually questioned you at dinner?"

"I don't like to advertise the fact. I have enough orders for scrimshaw without anymore."

"What about the two oriental men. Do you know what they were interested in?"

"I left when they arrived. I know nothing about them. I'll be out my investment won't I?"

Anthony grimaced. "Possibly."

"Anything else you would like to add?" Jim asked.

Ted shook his head.

"You may go, but don't leave Seattle just yet."

"Okay. How long will I be detained?"

We're not sure, but I will let you know when you can leave."

After Ted left the office, Jim asked Milton's and Anthony's impression of the questioning.

"In my opinion Ted is honest," Milton said.

"I agree. He seems honest."

After discussing the ivory's disappearance, Milton, Anthony and Jim reevaluated the suspects. They scrutinized each one singly. When they came to Bridgett and Bill, Milton reminded Jim they had seen them coming out of Tron's cabin.

Anthony snapped his fingers. "They have the ivory," he shouted.

"They have left the ship but were told to remain around for questioning," Jim said.

"Are they under surveillance?" Milton asked.

"No, they haven't been, but we can change that." Jim abruptly rose and left his office.

While he was gone, Milton and Anthony rehashed what they had been discussing. "Cornelia and Dave may have some ivory. The Captain let her take some for evaluation. Bridgett and Bill probably have some too."

"That means we could have two sets of thieves?"

177

"It appears that way," Milton said. "I don't believe Briana is as innocent as she seems. I'm not even sure that she was even pushed overboard."

"Could the entire incident have been staged?" Anthony tossed out the possibility.

"Sure why not? In fact, I believe the idea makes sense."

Anthony smiled. "Now, we're getting somewhere. Do you suppose Briana and Tron are stealing from her husband Dave and Cornelia?"

"Could be. Would they be that gutsy to take on Dave who may have attempted to kill Joe, his partner."

"And I know from experience, Cornelia is capable of the same," Anthony said emphatically.

Milton stroked his chin. "Is the ivory for their own benefit or just to foil Dave's plan?"

"Not sure." Anthony scowled. "Remember she does have a geology degree, so she can't be naive to the ivory trade."

"We must concentrate on Bridgett and Bill for answers. Just hope we're not too late."

Jim returned within fifteen minutes. "It's done. I've dispatched an officer to track down Bridgett and Bill. Now, we must wait." He rummaged in his desk drawer, pulled out some hard candy and passed it around.

Anthony unwrapped a piece and popped it into his mouth. "What do we do about the oriental men Cornelia was talking to?"

Jim massaged the stubble on his face. "I have men looking for them. They might have left the country by now."

"Cornelia is the only one who can answer that question, but I doubt if she'd talk. In my experience, she will be difficult to corner," Anthony said.

"Since both you two had dealings with Cornelia, I'd like you to be present when I question Cornelia," Jim said yawning.

"Go get something to eat. I'm in hopes we have someone to question by evening."

"No protests here. We'll be at the hotel," Anthony said.

"Without more ivory we have no case," Milton confided to Anthony as they left the building.

"So where is it?"

"I have an idea. What if the oriental men were more than customers?"

"You think they were working with Dave and Cornelia to move the goods?"

"Let's see if there were any security cameras operating in the dining room where they met."

Anthony clapped his partner on the back. "Could we be so lucky?"

Milton called Dora briefly and told her they would be by shortly for a quick afternoon bite to eat. Instead of returning straight to their rooms, they stopped off in the dining room. After showing their badges and being directed to the hotel manager, Milton explained the situation and what they were looking for. The manager affirmed that they did have a security camera but would need more verification before it could be turned over to the proper authorities.

Milton and Anthony joined their wives for an early evening meal while they waited for a call from Jim.

Dora fingered the rim of her cup. "I hope you will crack this case soon."

"Are you anxious to get home?" Milton asked her.

"I am, besides I want to know the whole story of the strange objects in the suitcase."

Anthony sighed. "We do too. But it seems no one will talk."

Milton buttered his dinner roll. "We have the suspects, but we must discover how they are all connected and what they did with the ivory."

While they were lingering over a pot of tea, Milton answered the expected call. "Jim wants us at the police station."

"We'll see you gals to the rooms before we go," Anthony reassured them as they scooted back their chairs in preparation to leave.

Milton paid the bill and after the women were safely deposited to their rooms, the men drove their borrowed vehicle to the station where they found Jim pacing the floor.

Jim pointed to the familiar chairs. "Have a seat."

Milton and Antony waited anxiously for news until he poured himself a cup of coffee.

"One of my men found a black suitcase in a dumpster. There are traces of fossil dust in it." Jim brought it out from a closet for inspection. "We have dusted for fingerprints. None found other than your wives and baggage handlers."

Milton stared at the empty suitcase. "So they transferred the contents to another place."

"There has to be more than what the suitcase could carry," Anthony added. "Otherwise it wouldn't be worth the trouble."

"I agree," Jim said. "Of course, merchandise can be sold and shipped. I believe this is where Cornelia comes in. As you know, we have nothing until we can find the contents of the suitcase."

"Cornelia is clever. She's not about to reveal where it is."

"True. That's why I'm not going to question her. She's too shrewd for that," Jim said. "Instead, we're going to interrogate Bill and Bridget. Tron worked for them. Briana is their granddaughter. They must know something."

Chapter Fourteen

Cornelia learned that Dave was in custody from Lee, one of her accomplices who sometimes worked as her backup and muscle man. She had hired him before the cruise. She chided herself for becoming involved with Dave. He was a professional paleontologist. "One would think he had a brain," she rambled to herself. She threw a magazine across her hotel room in disgust. Knowing by now that her accomplice Dave aka Otto had probably implicated her in the ivory theft, she knew she must act fast and disappear before she was called in for questioning. But first she had to locate the jade and the missing ivory. Having a hunch, she called Lee and asked him to locate the McFarlands.

In the meantime, she tossed the largest of her suitcases on the bed, opened it, and rummaged around for disguise accessories. She had been taught by the best, she told herself, as she set about her make-over. Choosing her black wig and ordinary street clothes, she quickly kicked off her high heels and removed her expensive clothes. She wiped off her make-up and donned a pair of oxfords, the plain clothes, and a pair of outdated, oval glasses.

Perusing the phone book for car rentals, she selected one nearest the hotel, checked out, and flagged a taxi to the rental company. She chose an inconspicuous compact model car and drove to the hotel where Bill and Bridgett were staying. By now, her man had not only located the hotel but also the room number of the McFarlands. So far, she felt confident no one was following her.

As she walked down the hall she noticed an empty champagne bottle by a door and snatched it.

Her heart beat wildly as she knocked on the door of the McFarland's hotel room. "Room service," she called out. A moment of silence followed.

"We didn't order anything."

"Compliments of Briana," she called back.

"Briana?" The door opened a crack. "I don't understand what did she send?"

"Champagne to celebrate."

"Well who are you?"

"I'm the concierge's assistant."

"Alright. Give me a moment." Bill unlatched the door and opened it wider. Cornelia rushed in before he could notice the bottle was empty. She slammed the door shut. Immediately, Bridgett gasped and stepped back.

"I want the ivory," she demanded. A light knock on the door alerted her to her backup, Lee, who had quickly slipped a mask over his face.

As soon as she let him in, he snatched their suitcases and opened them. Finding the ivory and the scrimshaw order there, he packed it up in a large suitcase he had brought with him while Cornelia stared down the couple. Afterwards, Lee tied and gagged them, and then he and Cornelia fled.

Cornelia assumed the driver's seat and sped to the dock area where their warehouse was located.

"Why are we going this way?" Lee asked in panic. "Don't you think we need to get out of this city?"

"We've got to warn them to move the ivory as quickly as possible. The cops we'll be on to us in a matter of time."

Lee didn't protest again. He had worked with Cornelia before and knew she always got her way.

Once they arrived, Cornelia lost no time in persuading the crew to work faster. The workmen were already loading the crates of ivory, disguised amongst the mammoth ivory, onto a ship. "When does the ship leave?" she asked.

"Tomorrow morning," one worker told her.

"That's not soon enough," Cornelia roared. "Otto, or should I say our illustrious paleontologist Dave, botched our plan."

"The ship should be on its way to China before anyone figures out what's going on," Lee said.

"Not according to the dock workers. I've been told plain clothes men have been snooping around. They have a good idea what's going on." Cornelia's tone turned icy.

Lee wrung his hands. "We can't do anything more here. I hope you have a plan for us."

"You forget. We have the scrimshaw order to deliver."

"Skip it," Lee advised. "It can't be worth much money. Saving ourselves is worth more."

This time, Cornelia listened to Him. "You're right. We'll unload it later. But in the meantime, we must get rid of this car."

———

The next day, Jim, Milton, and Anthony checked in with the dining room security. They were given permission to view the conversation with the two oriental men. Jim whisked the film to the police station where an identification check could be run on the two men. Just by watching the film, it was difficult to determine what was being said. While they were waiting for the results the three men discussed the case.

In the meantime, a call came in for Jim. By listening to the one-sided conversation, Milton determined something interesting had happened. Jim could barely contain his excitement when he hung up the phone.

"I sent a couple men to bring the McFarlands in for questioning. Wait until you hear this." Jim breathed in deeply. "When our officers got to the hotel, they knocked on the

McFarland's door but no one answered. Instead, they heard muffled noises in the room. After they got a key for the room, my men entered to find the couple tied up and gagged. It seems that Cornelia and a man entered and stole the ivory that the McFarlands had in their possession."

"What do you mean by seems?" Milton asked.

"The woman had black hair and her description didn't match the Cornelia you described."

"She's a master of disguise. It had to be her." Anthony frowned. "So she got away, again?"

"My men are checking out all the car rental places, the airport, the bus stations, and trains."

"How many hours start did they get on us?" Milton asked.

Jim shook his head. His enthusiasm dwindled. "That could be a problem. The McFarlands have been tied up for twelve hours."

"A good head start," Milton mused. "Are they okay?"

"Right now the doctors are checking them over."

"We'll do our best to find Cornelia and her side-kick. I'm hoping for a breakthrough with the security film."

The men reviewed the case from top to bottom until Jim was contacted about a possible match with the security film. According to the findings, one of the oriental men was identified as a suspect in other cases involving illegal elephant ivory trade although he was never convicted. Mammoth ivory was currently being used as a popular cover.

"There has to be more ivory stashed somewhere," Jim said. "The ivory and jade that was in the suitcase is a very small portion of this illegal activity."

"How is your warehouse surveillance coming?" Anthony asked.

"Haven't found anything yet, but these two men on the security camera could lead us to the big cache."

"And do you know where they are?"

"Not currently. We don't believe they have left the area yet."

"Anthony and I have been talking, and we are curious about the paleontology conference. Since Dave Gleason was a prominent part of it, we figure that the conference may have been a cover for the sale of mammoth ivory and perhaps elephant ivory."

"In what way?"

"Taking orders for the mammoth ivory that Dave and Joe procured in the tundra."

"So we should check all the conference attendees," Jim said. "I don't suppose anyone has the names except for Dave."

"Ted might be able to help us. Perhaps he remembered some attendees."

"Yeah, he did speak at the conference at least once," Anthony agreed.

"I'll bring Ted in for more questioning. Perhaps he'll remember the names of the two oriental men at the conference."

———

The next morning, Ted came into Jim's office, sat down, and fidgeted with his jacket until Jim appeared. He knew he hadn't done anything wrong and couldn't understand why the police were so interested in him.

"We need your help," Jim said.

Ted sat up straight. "I…um…I will try."

"Do you remember names of the conference attendees when you spoke that night?"

"I…I was introduced to several, but I have forgotten some of their names."

"Were you introduced to any Oriental men?"

"No."

"Oh," Jim said disappointed.

"You asked me about the Oriental men the first time I came in for questioning. Are they suspects?"

"Yes."

"Would you be able to tell me about anyone else who is a suspect? I'd like to know. Maybe I could help."

Jim thought a minute. "Yeah, sure. The major one is Dave Gleason."

Ted paled. "Dave Gleason? Oh, no."

"What's the matter?"

"Dave Gleason asked me to do some scrimshaw for him. He said his original scrimshaw artist was ill, and he had an order to fill. He seemed like a nice guy. We visited for quite a while after the conference. That's where he discovered I was a scrimshaw artist."

"I see," Jim mused. "Did you get paid for the order?"

"No. Dave never showed up to pay me."

"And where is the scrimshaw now?"

"I gave it to Bill McFarland per agreement when I finished my order."

"Why Bill McFarland?"

"I don't know. I just did what I was told and now I'm in trouble?"

"Not if you weren't aware of what you were doing was illegal?"

"And what was I doing?"

"We're not sure right at the moment, but why didn't you give us this information earlier?"

Ted shrugged. "I didn't think it important. I thought I was just helping someone out. Like I said I thought he was an okay guy."

"Do you know if the blanks you were using were mammoth, walrus, or elephant ivory?"

Ted shook his head. "I can't be certain, but I did suspect it was better quality than the mammoth ivory."

Jim also told him that Cornelia was the other suspect in the ivory case. He asked Ted if he remembered anything else about their meeting. Ted reiterated he had purchased a mammoth tusk, confirming the suspicion that more ivory was stored somewhere in Seattle. Jim told Ted to stick around Seattle for a while longer just in case they needed to ask him more questions. Before Ted left, he jotted down the names he remembered from the conference. Jim handed the list of names to his co-worker in hopes more connections could be made.

In an hour's time, the search of names resulted in a hit for a prior record. Lee Kenwick.

———

In the meantime, law enforcement commenced an all out search for Cornelia as well as stakeouts at the warehouses along the wharf.

Cornelia and Lee abandoned the rental car before they left Seattle and using one of her fake IDs, Cornelia picked up another rental at a different location. She and Lee traveled south all night in hopes of reaching California before the authorities stopped them for questioning. She had many connections and places to hide in California. But they were still many miles from safety.

Cornelia who normally had a countenance of steel panicked at any sign of law enforcement. Each patrol car sent her head to spinning. Cornelia wouldn't let Lee drive, so instead, he complained about every maneuver she made.

"I have a notion to drop you off by the side of the road if you don't shut up," she threatened him. "But you'd squeal on me."

"That I would. We're in this together, babe."

"Don't call me that," she screamed at him.

He held up his hands. "Get a grip. Don't lose it now."

Cornelia knew he had a point. She had to remain calm. Lee was no help in these situations and was only along for his muscle. He was a nice looking guy. The body builder type. But their romantic liaison hadn't lasted long. Wishing she had left him behind, she focused on their plight. Only one hundred miles to the California state line. She had connections in northern California. Only one problem, they must stop for gasoline.

Still dressed in her disguise, Cornelia volunteered to fill the tank with gas. Lee begged her to let him go in the convenience store for food. Against her better judgment, she agreed only if he disguised himself with a cap and dark glasses. "Keep your head down." She muttered under her breath that he was the typical food junkie.

"And don't run off and leave me." He shouted back.

Tempted to use her credit card, she thought better of it and opted to pay with cash. Besides, she wanted a cup of strong black coffee. As quickly as possible Cornelia and Lee left the store and stepped outside. Within seconds, patrol cars encircled them, and police lunged out of their vehicles, yelling orders to put their hands up. Cornelia dropped her coffee to the pavement.

———

In the evening, Jim asked Milton and Anthony to come along while he questioned Bill and Bridgett in the hospital. The couple had been badly shaken and was suffering from dehydration.

Jim ran his fingers through his disheveled hair. "I dislike being so callus, but I figure they will be in a vulnerable state and will be willing to talk."

An officer stationed outside the hospital room tipped his hat to the detectives. They entered the room where Bill and Bridgett had been assigned, hooked up to IV's. The television blared and the couple dozed. Bridgett startled when she heard the men at the door.

"Sorry, but we must ask you questions. Your honesty is vital," Jim said somberly. He reached for the control and turned the TV off.

"How's Briana?" Bridgett asked close to tears.

"She's in custody and has a lot of explaining to do. You can help her by telling us the truth."

Bridgett struggled to sit up and looked to Bill. He sighed and nodded. "Okay, what do you want to know?"

"Everything. Start at the beginning." The three men pulled up chairs, sat down, and waited for Bill to begin.

Bill cleared his throat and said wearily, "If Dave wouldn't have bought Briana a drink in the bar that night, we wouldn't be here now. Dave has been nothing but trouble."

"How so?"

Bridgett assumed the rest of the conversation. "He played us for fools. He never loved Briana. We had money, and that was what he was after."

Jim decided not to interrupt Bridgett's dialogue unless she faltered. According to her, Briana met Dave at a swanky New York bar and Dave swept her up by pretending to be a charming paleontologist. In less than six months, they married at the McFarland mansion. All seemed well for two more months until Dave planned a series of business trips keeping him from home for weeks at a time. Briana had been unhappy and jumped at the chance to accompany Dave on a cruise to Alaska. She knew he would be busy at the seminar, but she hoped she could spend some time with him.

Bridgett pause and drank a few sips of water. "Bill and I didn't care for him from the very start. To us he seemed like an opportunist, but we loaned him money for a business venture. I suppose it was for his ivory debacle."

Bridgett further commented that Tron had been working for them as their butler when Briana and Dave were dating. Sometime after their wedding, Tron left without an explanation. "We trusted him explicitly," Bridgett added.

Bill interrupted and explained he had been the jewelry business for years and had learned to carve scrimshaw as an apprentice. Briana had apparently let that information slip when Dave had questioned her about her grandfather's business affairs. Dave had asked Bill and Bridgett to accompany them on the cruise. At the time Bill didn't know he would be asked to carve ivory to fill Dave's order.

"We were happy to go, so we could keep an eye on Briana. At the time, she was depressed about her marriage and suspected he was involved with another woman. It was only later after Briana fell overboard, he asked me to carve ivory for him."

"Did she fall overboard," Jim asked pointedly.

Bill squirmed. "No. My wife and I along with Tron and Briana staged the entire incident. Briana suspected her husband was involved in something illegal and was afraid for her life. She wanted to draw attention and implicate him in his illegal scheme."

"She did a good job at that," Milton commented.

"We were hoping Dave believed that she actually fell overboard and drowned. It was our way of protecting her."

"Why did you say yes to the scrimshaw?" Jim asked.

"I was afraid of Dave. He approached me as I had no other choice, and I was fearful for Briana."

"You knew where Briana was all along?"

"We did. Tron said he would take care of her."

Jim scratched his head. "I'm puzzled why Briana took the ivory cache from Dora's sewing locker?"

Bill chuckled. "Briana is a spirited one. She did it to aggravate Dave. Of course, he never found out."

"Were you going to keep the cache?"

"We didn't think that far ahead, but your suspects have it now."

Chapter Fifteen

Early in the morning of the following day, Cornelia was brought in for questioning. During the four hours of interrogation, Cornelia refused to cooperate. She had worn Jim down to a frazzle. He called Milton and Anthony to assist. "You have worked with her before," he said.

Anthony volunteered to deal with her first. "Are you sure?" Milton asked, remembering San Cruz and Anthony's near drowning. Anthony was sure Cornelia intended to do him in.

"Yes, I'd like to see her squirm."

As soon as Anthony entered the room, Cornelia batted her eyes and said, "Tony, what do I owe this honor?"

"We meet again. Funny how we seem to cross paths."

"You should know by now if you cooperate you may get a break."

"I don't know what you're talking about. I have done nothing wrong."

Anthony did his best to wear her down but no matter what he said, she outmaneuvered him. Finally, he gave up and left Cornelia behind, smirking.

In defeat, he returned to the office and offered Milton a chance at breaking her down.

"Let's question Lee," Milton suggested. "I have a hunch we can crack him. Cornelia will never budge."

Jim agreed and called Lee in for questioning. He held out for three hours and finally caved, spilling the information most needed. From him, the investigative team learned a ship was on its way to China with the illegal ivory. The two oriental men no doubt were on the ship, too.

Immediately, Jim dispatched the information to the port authorities. Someone would be there when the ship docked in China.

"No need to question Cornelia," Jim told Milton and Anthony. "We have all the evidence we need for now. Once the ship docks, we will have everything necessary to make a conviction."

"This time Cornelia will pay her dues," Anthony cheered with satisfaction.

———

In the late afternoon, Jim thanked Milton and Anthony profusely for their assistance but told them he and his police force would be able to tie up the loose ends. The two detectives lost no time in joining their wives at the hotel for the evening. Milton called ahead to let them know their part in the case had been concluded.

Before they went down to the dining room for the evening meal, the wives greeted them with smiles and open arms. They wanted to hear the entire story and asked questions.

"What will happen to Bridgett and Bill?" Josie asked.

"They aren't entirely exonerated," Milton said. "They did stage an accident and withheld information on Briana and Tron's disappearance."

"Briana and Tron aren't pardoned, either on the supposed drowning incident," Anthony added.

"Ted is innocent, isn't he?" Dora asked.

Milton nodded. "I believe so. He had no knowledge he was working with criminals."

"Good. I liked him."

Josie raised her hand. "Who was the inside man permitting the black suitcase from being scanned?"

"That would be Lee," Anthony answered. "He worked as a baggage handler and also had access to the keys."

"And there's the issue of Briana's quilt," Dora said. "Who brought it to the quilt show?"

"Briana admitted she asked a staff member to take it to the show."

"But why?"

"To let you know she was okay."

"Really? Dora touched her cheek. "I had no idea she would care. She did take the ivory staff from my sewing locker."

Milton smiled. "Briana was a victim, too. She didn't want her criminal husband to have it."

Dora trembled. "She was playing a dangerous game."

When the questions ceased," Milton suggested they go downstairs for dinner. "We have something else to discuss," he told the women.

Dora cringed. "We don't have to stay here any longer, do we?"

Milton laughed softly. "No, we don't. You'll like what we have to say."

"Hope it's not another cruise," Josie said under her breath.

Anthony laughed, flagged down a waiter, and ordered a bottle of wine. "We must celebrate."

Dora glowered. "That we survived another crime?"

"Yes, and the fact the scoundrels have been brought to justice."

Josie glanced at Dora and scowled. "Give credit where credit is due."

"Now ladies. Let's not become testy. True, we have been under a lot of unnecessary stress, and I admire you lovely ladies for handling it so well." Milton cleared his throat. "In fact, that's what Anthony and I want to talk about. Anthony, would you do the honors?"

"Wait," Josie held up her palms. "You bought us jewelry to make up for the botched vacation."

"It's not carved ivory, is it?" Dora asked.

Anthony smiled. "It's even better than that. Any more guesses?"

Dora shrugged seemingly not in the mood for guessing games.

"Milton and I have decided to retire."

"Are you serious?" Dora demanded. "No more detectives?"

Milton nodded and reached across the table to pat her hand. "We have put you through enough intrigue for a lifetime. You have been good sports but enough is enough."

Dora sighed. "I agree. Both Josie and I vowed we would not accompany you two on anymore assignments."

Anthony laughed. "We don't blame you at all."

The couples lifted their wine glasses to toast the adventures of yesterday and the peace and quiet of tomorrow.

Milton grinned and then blew Dora a kiss. "But it was worth it."

Dora's face began to form into her typical scowl and then relaxed into a sparkling smile.

Books in the Winslow Quilting Mysteries Series

Heist Along the Rails
The Library Quilt Caper
Clues in the Civil War Album
The Nativity Quilt
The Quilting Cruise Gambit